PENGUIN METR

HEART ON THE EDGE

Novoneel Chakraborty is the prolific author of fifteen bestselling thriller novels, two e-novellas and one bestselling short story collection, with his works being translated into multiple Indian languages. Almost all his novels have debuted in the top three Nielsen listings across India and have continued to be in the top positions on various bestseller lists for several months after release.

His Forever series made it to the *Times of India's* Most Stunning Books of 2017 list, while the Stranger trilogy became a phenomenal hit among young adults, with Amazon tagging it, along with his erotic thriller *Black Suits You*, as their memorable reads of the year. He has sold over 1 million copies and is India's most popular thriller novelist.

His latest releases, *Cross Your Heart, Take My Name; Roses Are Blood Red; Whisper to Me Your Lies* and *A Thousand Kisses Deep* are still in the top ten list across India. His twists, dark plots and strong female protagonists have earned him the moniker 'Sidney Sheldon of India'.

The Stranger trilogy, his immensely popular thriller series, has been translated into six Indian languages. The trilogy has also been adapted into a successful web series by Applause Entertainment on MX Player, amassing a whopping 600 million-plus views. Other successful adaptations for the screen include *Black Suits You* and the Forever series.

Novoneel has written several hit TV and original web shows for premier channels like MX Player, Sony, Star Plus, Zee and Zee5. He lives and works in Mumbai.

ALSO BY THE SAME AUTHOR

HEART ON THE EDGE

NOVONEEL CHAKRABORTY

Penguin
metro reads

An imprint of Penguin Random House

PENGUIN METRO READS

USA | Canada | UK | Ireland | Australia
New Zealand | India | South Africa | China

Penguin Metro Reads is part of the Penguin Random House group of companies
whose addresses can be found at global.penguinrandomhouse.com

Published by Penguin Random House India Pvt. Ltd
4th Floor, Capital Tower 1, MG Road,
Gurugram 122 002, Haryana, India

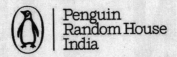

Penguin
Random House
India

First published in Penguin Metro Reads by Penguin Random House India 2022

ISBN 9780143449515

Typeset in Requiem Text and Bembo Std by MAP Systems, Bengaluru, India
Printed at Replika Press Pvt. Ltd, India

www.penguin.co.in

MIX
Paper from
responsible sources
FSC® C016779

For every elder sibling out there

Prologue: The Wronged One

Revenge seldom happens the way it's shown in the movies. The main difference is that a movie has a certain time limit within which everything has to be done. In reality, you have your entire life in front of you. Of course, a movie has an audience. Life doesn't have an audience. It only has you—the wronged one.

The worst gift of a childhood trauma to you is that it never allows you to live a normal life. Ever. Either it screws your emotional self. Or your social behaviour. Worse, both. The trauma becomes this bridge of hell between your past childhood and your present adult life. It doesn't let you either cross that bridge or lay off it. The trauma itself becomes the centre stage of your being. And everything that you think, you do, you desire, you fear, you love . . . all of it is a result of that trauma. You seek that one thing, or a person who can be the magical eraser, removing the trauma from your core, but those things, again, happen in the movies. The only way to heal the trauma is acceptance. Easier said than done.

Acceptance is a tricky thing because there are two facets to it. And more often than not, we think acceptance is the first cousin of forgiveness. On the contrary, it isn't. Acceptance means you've finally made peace with the fact that you can't alter what happened in the past. The other facet is that acceptance may not necessarily mean you have moved on though, that you have freed yourself from the heavy shackles of the trauma. Forgiveness, sometimes, is a defence mechanism. Revenge is an attack mechanism.

When I look in the mirror, I don't recognize myself. And it's not something that has happened over one day or a week or a month or even a year. It's close to two decades. What pains me is that I'm not what I should have become. I'm what the trauma manipulated me to become. I'm biologically a woman but I haven't had normal menses ever. It has led to constant suffering for years. But in these many years, I haven't for once asked god why he made me a woman. I just curse god every day for making men the way he did. It's such a gross blunder. I think god was happy creating only women. But then he thought, how would the world produce more women? So, he created men. And men made sure there were more men than women in the world. And the ones there were, never could step up to their shoulder level, ever.

My own experience tells me that there's still a limit to a human's goodness but, I dare say, there's no limit to a human's dark, twisted mind. It's a bottomless pit. It's because of this that the entire legal system was created. To check that 'pit'. Every time I think humans won't surprise me any more with their dark shit, something comes up that raises the morbid bar. It's everywhere. You open the newspapers, you turn on the news channels, you look around when you move out. It's a jungle out there with rules for the powerful to chuck the rules. What about the ones who get squashed? Who get emotionally nihilated? Who get irreversibly traumatized?

Right now, as I stand on the balcony of my house, I take a deep breath in. And count to four before releasing it slowly. I can feel a storm is about to hit a lot of people.

I'm ready, I tell myself.

Chapter 1

Within the several houses in one of the small localities of Karur, Tamil Nadu, it was that time of the day when the Internet connection was at its peak. There was a certain time, between 11.30 a.m. and 1 p.m., on alternate days, which the local people used to call 'the download hour'. The Internet strength at that time allowed a maximum download speed. And Shravan Kamaraj always made sure that he was in front of the desktop computer in his room at that time. Shravan was studying in standard twelve. At his age, he showed a really high emotional quotient (EQ). Unlike most of his friends at school, Shravan was always kind to animals and plants, for which he was mocked many times.

The computer wasn't bought for him, though. It was bought for his elder sister, Naishee, when she was in standard twelve. She had not let him touch it except for his school projects, but now it was all his. There were times when Shravan used to lament, in a silly manner, the fact that he was born after Naishee. Else, he would have enjoyed everything brand-new. Hailing from a middle-class family, most of Shravan's toys, books, etc., had been used by Naishee first. But he never held it against Naishee since he loved his sister to death. She was his confidante and best friend.

The moment the download hour hit, Shravan was ready in front of the computer. He was totally engrossed in the video that he was watching. It was playing without buffering for once and the quality was 1080HD. His engagement, however, was cut short when he heard the doorbell of their house ring thrice, at one go. Shravan was irked but he knew quite well who did that. *Akka!* His elder sister. He didn't stop to switch off what he was watching on the computer. With a joyful smile and brewing excitement, Shravan ran out of his room impulsively, took the stairs down and then almost flung himself on to the main door. His mother, Meenakshi Kamaraj, too had come out of the kitchen with equal eagerness. Shravan opened the door with a sly smile as if he didn't want to tell his sister that he was surprised. His smile further stretched seeing his akka with her luggage and with AirPods on.

Shravan hugged her tight. Naishee tried to push him away.

'Chee! You're sweating. Stay away, piggy!' she said and stepped in.

'One piggy doesn't need to clean up while meeting another piggy,' Shravan shot back. It was their usual banter. Both respected and loved each other, but when they opened their mouths, they addressed each other as one animal or the other.

'And when did you buy these AirPods? You never told me!'

'You're *appa* or what? I don't need to tell you anything.'

Shravan made a face but quickly took her luggage inside and closed the door.

'I had a feeling you would drop in,' Meenakshi said, as Naishee gave her a hug and a peck on her cheek.

'Can't you ever inform us before coming?' Shravan asked.

'Shut up. Do I have to remind you that I came before you? So, no, I don't have to inform you about anything. In fact, it's you who has to inform me about everything, every time.' Naishee went close to Shravan, held his hair and pulled it forcefully.

'And even if I did inform you, would you have prepared a red carpet for me?' She let go of his hair.

It was a Saturday. Naishee had done this before as well. She used to live in Hyderabad. At least that's what her parents thought. Only Shravan knew the truth. She had come from Bengaluru.

Naishee was an engineering graduate who had secured a campus recruitment at Deloitte. She worked there for three years, saved a little and then one day resigned. It was in the third year of college that she had picked up a hobby—photography—from her then-boyfriend. The relationship didn't last; the hobby did. It became a passion by the time she joined Deloitte. *Perhaps he came into my life to give me my passion*, Naishee often wondered whenever thoughts of her ex plagued her. While her father, Mani Kamaraj, wanted her to pursue an MBA, Naishee took a small loan while working to pay for an advanced distance-photography course from a university abroad, without letting her parents know.

Initially, even Shravan didn't know about it. When he started checking out Naishee's photography page on Instagram, he couldn't take his eyes off it. He recommended that she become a professional photographer. It was then that she let him know the truth. That she not only had completed a professional photography course but also had resigned from Deloitte. Currently, Naishee was working as the head director of photography (DOP) with a wedding planning and event management company in Bengaluru. Her parents, though, thought she was still working at Deloitte, in Hyderabad.

'Where's appa?' Naishee asked her mother, after breaking from her hug. She had been a silent spectator during the sibling banter and watched them with a smile. Every time she saw the two together, she wondered when they had grown up. And that some of their traits never changed even if they were grown-ups now. As Naishee headed towards the kitchen leaving Shravan

3

behind, he got busy sorting his hair. The kitchen was on the ground floor.

'He has gone to the terrace to dry the washed clothes. Maybe he didn't hear the doorbell. Go and surprise him,' Meenakshi said, joining her daughter in the kitchen. Naishee moved out and took the stairs. Following her, Shravan too rushed for his room. It just struck him that moment that he had committed a blunder. And he had hardly any time to rectify it.

'Akka, wait!' Shravan blurted out, running after her.

While Naishee climbed the set of extra stairs that led to the terrace, Shravan rushed inside his room. And stopped still.

'Appa?' Naishee reached the terrace. She called out a couple of times more, but her father didn't respond. This had never happened before. Her father loved her so much that it was always a race between Shravan and him as to who would open the door when she pressed the doorbell in her style.

Naishee ambled to the middle of the terrace. There was a small raised cemented platform. It was her favourite place at home. Naishee had spent so many nights alone here, sitting atop it, looking admiringly at the night sky. She climbed the platform and took a deep breath. She felt happy from within. Happiness in life is about one's choices. And she was happy that at twenty-five, she had made her choices without worrying about the consequences as such. Her trance was broken by a sharp cry from Shravan. Then, she heard her father bellow out loud.

Naishee quickly dashed from the terrace and reached the floor downstairs in no time. It was the floor where their bedrooms were. She found her father in Shravan's room. As she stood by the door, her mother appeared behind her. Both women looked at the two men in the family. One looked enraged. The other looked embarrassed.

'What happened, appa?' Naishee asked.

'Ask your brother,' he said curtly, gesturing towards the desktop computer. Naishee had seen her father livid after a long time. She tiptoed towards the computer and glanced at it.

After a few seconds of staring at the computer, she realized that her weekend holiday had been ruined. Now, all hell was about to break loose.

* * *

Chapter 2

What followed was the worst crisis in the Kamaraj house ever. And the duty to resolve it fell on Naishee's shoulders. The problem wasn't that her father had found out that Shravan was watching porn. It was the fact that he was watching gay porn, to be specific. This wasn't the first time Mani had noticed his son's inclination towards men.

Before this, Mani had, in his words, caught Shravan in Naishee's old dresses a few times. He had scolded him for it. He'd caught him once masturbating, looking at the paused image of a male Tamil movie star. But the actress was also in the frame so Mani couldn't be sure. He understood his son was growing up and had subtly asked him to relieve himself in the washroom. The latest was three weeks back when Meenakshi told him that she had seen Shravan waxing his legs. She was so taken aback that she didn't even confront her son about it. And now, this. In his regressive mind, Mani had already accepted that there was something terribly wrong with his son. He lambasted Shravan for a good one hour. Naishee did try to calm Mani down but he didn't listen. In the end, he turned towards Naishee and asked her to explain to her brother how to become 'normal'. While Mani did his usual thing of walking out of the house whenever he was angry, Shravan went and locked himself on the terrace. Naishee tried her best to coax him to talk but Shravan didn't budge. She chose to give him the space he needed. Shravan even skipped lunch. Meenakshi was worried for her son for the entire day but Naishee calmed her down. She knew her brother better than most.

'He will call me,' she told Meenakshi with conviction. And that's what happened a little after she had a quiet dinner with her parents. Naishee knew her father—someone from whom she had to hide the fact that she was following her passion—wouldn't understand that even if Shravan showed gay tendencies, it was all right. His parenting was otherwise good, but Mani had tried his best to instil the same middle-class insecurities that he had probably soaked in from his parents. Running after 'security' was what a quintessential middle-class person was all about. And then they called the sordid, monotonous loop—life!

Naishee was constantly checking her phone for Shravan's message. When it came, Naishee quickly took some idli, which her mother had prepared, along with some sambhar in a bowl and went to the terrace. Her parents noticed it but didn't say anything.

Naishee had to knock twice before Shravan opened the terrace door. She stepped in, and he locked it again. Then he went and sat on the cemented platform. She followed him. For the first few minutes, there was no talk between them.

'Hey doggy, I can't hold this for long. Amma has surpassed herself in taste today—'

Naishee had barely finished speaking when Shravan snatched the bowl from her. In no time, he had gobbled it all. Looking at him, Naishee realized how hungry he must have been. A part of her was sad as well, seeing her brother this way.

'You have always been stupid. No matter how angry or upset I am, have you ever seen me skipping food?' Naishee said. There was the elder-sister concern in her voice. This time she pulled Shravan's hair playfully. Then noticed he had moist eyes.

'I need to confess something, akka,' he said. Naishee's silence egged him on.

'I'm gay, akka. Is it wrong?' His body was shuddering. Though Naishee had an inkling about the same thing, this was the first time she was hearing her brother say it out loud. There were many instances—small ones, big ones—when she understood Shravan's inclination towards boys, but she didn't probe him about it. It was his personal matter, after all. More importantly, he wasn't an adult then. Now he was eighteen years old. He had the moral right to be what he wanted to be. The one thing she hadn't anticipated, which was now the root of the tension at home, was that this would come out in the open to her parents this soon. And in a disastrous way.

'Listen, Murali—' Shravan knew that whenever Naishee called him by his nickname, she had something concrete in mind. He let her continue.

'Doesn't matter where life throws us, we always have two options: One, the obvious way. Second, the smart way. The obvious option for you here is to go against appa and stick with what you think is right. The smart way, however, is for you to keep quiet, let appa assume you are doing what he wants you to do and then live as per your choice once you start earning.'

Shravan took some time to consume what his akka said. It made sense to him. One of the reasons his parents loved Naishee was because she never compromised on the image that she was the perfect daughter to them, who lived the way they wanted her to. Whereas the truth was, they didn't know that she never lived by their rules. This was something Shravan could never do. He was more expressive with his choices. He could never lie. He'd heard Naishee say many times in the past, 'To lie in order to experience a bigger truth is totally all right.'

'So, what do you suggest?' he asked.

Half an hour later, Shravan and Naishee came down from the terrace together. Mani and Meenakshi were in the hall room. The news was playing on the TV. Mani still seemed to be fuming. Meenakshi looked concerned sensing her children were standing by the hall room door. Naishee came in first. Shravan followed. He was trembling as he always did in front of his father. Mani was sipping some hot milk while watching the news intently. He was aware of the two coming into the room.

'Appa?' Shravan said, in a fragile voice. Mani lifted his head, glanced at him once and put his glasses down on the table in front of him with a thud.

'I'm sorry, appa. This won't happen again. It's just a phase. And it's gone now.'

Mani remained quiet. As per the siblings' plan, if their father didn't speak, Naishee would speak up. And she did.

'Appa, Shravan has understood how wrong he is. I've explained it to him. Chapter closed. I'm here only for the weekend. I didn't come here to see grim faces. Come on now!'

Meenakshi gestured to Mani to forgive their son. When Mani wasn't looking, Naishee gestured to Shravan to plead with his father. Shravan immediately went and fell at Mani's feet and apologized again. Mani felt awkward, but he picked Shravan up and hugged him tightly.

'When will your generation understand what we say is for your own good,' Mani said and didn't stop there.

As Mani started his regressive lecture on why it was a sin for Shravan to watch such videos and also to think he was gay, Shravan glanced at Naishee. The latter winked at him. Both kept listening to their father's lecture like obedient kids.

Naishee's phone buzzed with a notification in-between. She tapped it. There was a message with a timer. She was in two minds whether she should open it now or . . . She did open it. And knew she shouldn't have. It was a dick pic.

* * *

Chapter 3

It was during her bus drive back to Bengaluru, after telling her parents that she was going to Hyderabad, that Naishee finally got some time to focus on her state of mind since she had received the pic message. The dick pic had made her blood rush as well. It wasn't just the dick pic, though. It was about the person who had written 'N' on it with whipped cream and then sent the pic to her. It was not the first time even, that Ashwath had done something like that. There was an inherent naughtiness in him that she adored. But that was only the last in the list of traits that had made Naishee fall for him.

Naishee was pretty clear after her heartbreak in her final year of engineering, that she wouldn't get involved with any guy ever again. The typical human behaviour after a bad break-up. It was the clichéd betrayal that had happened to her. She had met the guy in her first year. He was two years her senior. A bout of ragging led him to propose to her. Naishee said 'yes' out of fear. But then his love, care and possessiveness made her fall head-over-heels for him. The same way an eighteen-year-old girl, away from her father's tutelage, tries to find a father figure in her boyfriend. That's exactly what had happened with her then. Now when she looked back, every act of his was toxic but back then she labelled them as acts of true love. Naishee used to laugh at it all whenever she thought about it. And when you laugh at your own past, you know for a fact that you have grown. The past isn't something you'd rue. It is there so one can draw wisdom out of it and add it to one's personal evolution.

Ashwath wasn't someone she had discovered on her own. He was thrust upon her by her parents. He was the son of one of her father's friends with whom Mani had connected after Shravan had created a Facebook profile for both his mother and father. When Naishee came to know about it, she had personally beaten Shravan up for one hour. But the damage had been done by then. Naishee had to meet Ashwath.

She had taken his phone number from her father and got on a bus to Hyderabad from Bengaluru. Ashwath was working as a software engineer in an American MNC. Naishee had to project to him that she was working at Deloitte in Hyderabad; hence, she chose a weekend to meet up. They met at City Centre Mall for lunch. She had gone there to request him to say no to whatever their respective parents were cooking up in their minds, but she was in for a surprise herself. The first common ground she found with Ashwath was that he too had a secret alternate career. He was a stand-up comic. He hadn't given up on his job, but talking to Naishee he felt inspired. Especially after learning, in due course of their conversation, that she actually lived in Bengaluru. Naishee hadn't planned to blurt out her secret, but as they say, when you meet the person, you meet the person.

'I don't know if we both will have a future together or not, but I'll never forget you.' This was Ashwath's parting line to Naishee after their first meeting. He went back and told his parents that he liked her while she went back and told her parents she wouldn't mind meeting him again, contrary to what she had had in mind before. What clicked with Naishee was the fact that a man was keeping her at the centre of his inspiration. It was an emotional kick for her. And a first. Whatever little doubts she had about whether Ashwath was being truthful or simply trying to get in her good books were removed during their second meeting a month later.

'What's this?' Naishee asked. They were meeting at the same mall. Ashwath had turned his phone to show her an email. As Naishee read it, she understood it was his resignation email.

'You resigned?' She couldn't suppress her surprise.

'You are to be blamed. I always wanted to do this but never had the courage.'

'Fear of parents?'

'That. And fear of the unknown as well. It's all right to follow one's passion, but what if you don't succeed at it? I mean, success is important, right?'

'It is, indeed. But it also depends on how you define success. Is it fame? Is it money? Is it societal ticks? Or is it the joy you feel by simply doing what you love the most? Like I'm in love with photography. So, all I seek is a good photograph. Of course, I need money to sustain my passion. Thus I don't indulge in any kind of insane spending. That's me.'

There was an awkward silence. The way Ashwath was staring at Naishee, she felt uncomfortable.

'What? Say it, don't just stare. Staring at anyone like this is indecent.' She shrugged.

'Where were you all this while? We should have met long ago.'

Naishee burst out laughing. Every relationship has a moment when its destiny is decided. This was the moment when Naishee and Ashwath's destiny was decided—that they would be together. He took her to his stand-up act later that evening. He opened the night for the star stand-up comic there. She loved his act and told him that he had promise but obviously needed to work harder. Instead of being happy that he had a girl in his life, he felt happier that he had someone who was honest with him. By then, Ashwath knew one could get a girlfriend in life, but to get someone with whom you could be absolutely honest and emotionally naked was rare. Unlike Naishee, he had never had any bad relationships in the past. But, neither had he had any serious relationships either.

'I know I can be an asshole at times, but I have a request,' Ashwath said, during one of their dates. By then, the respective parents knew the two had crossed the first phase.

'That I suffer your assholic nature without complaints? I'm sorry I won't be—'

'No! That even if we don't click as a couple, you will be around as a friend.'

The request seemed so genuine that Naishee couldn't help but nod. Thankfully for Ashwath, they didn't have to be just friends. When he expressed his desire to visit Bengaluru, Naishee didn't mind. They met at Toit, chit-chatted over beer, and when the time came for them to leave, he was drunk.

'I don't think it's a good idea to drive back in this state,' he said.

'You could have told me straight you wanted to stay back. I don't mind.'

Ashwath smiled and noted the pros of dating a smart girl. When they reached her home neither had to speak much. Both knew why they were there. An hour of relentless love-making later, when they collapsed beside each other on her bed, naked, Naishee took some time before she said, 'Don't think this sex was a coincidence. I wanted to check if our sexual compatibility was all right. Don't want to be that lady in her thirties or forties whose husband can't satisfy her and she seeks out other men on social media.'

'Wow. Thanks. So, are we compatible?' Ashwath asked. He could see only the silhouette of her back since she hadn't let him switch the lights on. He saw her turn towards him.

'First, answer this, when are we fucking next?' Naishee asked, grabbing his balls. Ashwath couldn't help but laugh loudly at first before shrieking out in pain as she squeezed them.

Ashwath drove off to Hyderabad the following morning. When two weekends later Naishee dropped into her home, the dick pic was a signal. Naishee took a bus to Bengaluru while Ashwath drove there from Hyderabad the next day. They were constantly in touch with each other. It ended only when he parked the car and entered her apartment.

The moment he came in, Naishee pulled him to her and unleashed herself. He loved the way she wanted to dominate him always. That he didn't have to exhibit his alpha-ness all the time. It was in the middle of their act that Naishee's phone rang. Once. Twice. Thrice. Somehow it disturbed their sexual rhythm.

'Can't you just put it on silent?' Ashwath lamented, sucking her boobs alternately. Naishee was riding him. She stopped and sat up straight, which took her boobs away from him. She looked around to spot her phone at some distance on the bed. She stretched and picked it up. She noticed all the calls were from her mother. Naishee frowned. Instead of returning her focus to Ashwath, who was waiting for her to continue riding him, she decided to call her mother back, getting up from him. Afraid he would lose his erection, Ashwath was about to speak when Naishee gestured for him to be quiet.

'Hello, amma, what happened?'

'Shravan is nowhere to be found.' Meenakshi's voice was shaking.

* * *

Chapter 4

It took close to eight hours for Naishee to leave her apartment in Bengaluru, take a bus and reach her house in Karur. Ashwath had asked if he should accompany her and drive her there. Naishee asked him to leave for Hyderabad instead. She didn't want her parents to think that they were constantly together. Her parents had this amazing talent of making a mountain out of a molehill even though they were the ones who brought Ashwath into her life.

From the moment Naishee received the phone call, Ashwath could read the tension in her eyes. He didn't even ask her if they should complete what they were doing. As Naishee ended the call and sat looking worried, he realized there was a sudden nervous energy about her. Covering her naked body with the blanket, he held her tight in his embrace. He noticed her wiping her eyes and allowed her the comfort of silence. Whatever he knew of Naishee, Ashwath was sure she was a strong girl. And if something had made her shudder, it must be very serious.

'Calm down. Tell me what happened,' Ashwath said.

'My brother, Shravan, he is missing,' she said.

'What? He must have gone to some friend's place.'

'It's been more than twenty-four hours now. My parents didn't tell me before because they thought he would be back, but he isn't.'

'You want me to come with you?' Ashwath asked. Then he watched Naishee free herself from their embrace, get dressed, pack her stuff and then come to him.

'I guess I'll leave now. Sorry for this mess.'

'Hey, it's all right. I can—'

'Please don't. It's my battle. I hate to depend on others. But I'll let you know if I need you. That's a promise.'

Naishee pecked him on his cheeks.

'Switch off the lights and fans when you leave,' she said and left the flat. Ashwath took a deep breath and wrapped up as well.

The moment Naishee reached her home, she could feel the sombre mood. Never before had her home visit felt that way. Her mother opened the main door and started crying, holding her.

'Amma, calm down. Let's go inside first.'

As Naishee entered the hall, she noticed her father sitting all nervous and edgy. There were people from the locality. There were Mr and Mrs Sitaraman, their neighbours; Dr Laxmi Vishwanathan, the local doctor; Anju George, a tutor; Mohan Iyer, the grocery storekeeper; and Arthi Raman, a teacher who used to live in the locality and taught in the school where Shravan studied.

Naishee greeted them one by one. They all took their leave soon. Once they went out of the house, Naishee went to her father.

'Did you say anything to him, appa?'

'What? No. I didn't say anything. What would I say?'

'About him being gay.' Naishee wasn't mincing her words.

'But he isn't gay. He only came and told me the other day.' Mani threw a confused glance at his wife. Then at Naishee.

'Have you called all his friends?' Naishee moved to the sofa.

'Yes. I've also filed a missing person report with the police,' Mani said, as Naishee sat down opposite him.

'What did they say?'

'They will get back to us if they find anything. They have taken Shravan's photograph.'

'When was the last time you saw him?' Naishee looked at her mother first.

'The day before yesterday. I had asked him to get some bread.'

'What time?'

'Six in the evening or so,' Meenakshi said and started crying. 'I shouldn't have sent him.' Naishee went to her mother and calmed her down.

'Where's his phone?'

'It wasn't at home so we assumed he had taken it with him,' Mani cut in.

'Can't the police track his phone?'

Both her parents were quiet. Then Mani spoke.

'Let me visit them once today.' He stood up and walked out of the hall. Naishee and Meenakshi heard the door open and close.

Mani came back from the police station two hours later. The women had not moved from their seats.

'The police did track his phone's last location. And . . .'

The pause seemed claustrophobic to Naishee.

'It seems he went to Bengaluru.'

Naishee frowned. Why would Shravan go to Bengaluru? Was he trying to get in touch with her? Only he knew she was in that city. But then why didn't he call or message? And why would he travel when he was asked to buy bread? It sounded absurd.

'Have they sent a police team to Bengaluru?' Meenakshi asked.

'No.'

'What?' Naishee looked flabbergasted. 'Why not?'

'They think Shravan must have gone of his own accord. He is eighteen and will return if he wants to.'

'What rubbish! Why would they think so?' Naishee asked.

Mani, with an apologetic face, said, 'I'd told them about our fight. I lied about the reason though. I told them I had scolded him about his poor marks.'

'This is the limit, appa. Shravan is missing and you are still ashamed of him?' Naishee stood up and dashed towards the staircase. The house reverberated with the sound of her heavy steps until she went inside her room and closed the door with a thud.

It was late at night when Naishee received a call from Ashwath. Though she saw his messages coming in on WhatsApp, she wasn't in the mood to respond. The only message she had sent him was that she'd reached home safely. This time, though, she took the call.

'I'm really sorry, Ash—'

'Come to the terrace,' she heard him cut her short.

'What?' Naishee quickly moved out of her bed and rushed to the terrace. She looked down at a phone's flashlight waving at her.

'What the fuck! Who told you where I lived?' Naishee asked on the phone, looking down at him.

'No one.' There was a pause. Naishee heard heavy breathing as if Ashwath was thinking hard to himself. Then he said, 'I had followed you the day you came here on the weekend.'

Naishee didn't know how to react to that.

* * *

Chapter 5

Though the two were on call, they could see each other. Ashwath was still on the road. He had switched off his phone's flashlight. Naishee was on the terrace of her house speaking in whispers and still feeling she was being loud. The neighbourhood, as it did every day, slept early. Even the stray dogs weren't awake.

'You're creeping me out, Ashwath,' Naishee said on the phone. Her heart was still beating fast.

'I'm sorry if I am. I can understand, but—'

'But what, Ashwath? Why on earth would you follow me to my home?' Naishee had never, ever felt Ashwath had any creepy or stalker vibe. They did play the stalker fantasy a few times in bed but that was just roleplay. Or so Naishee had assumed.

'Come in,' Naishee said. She ended the call. Though Ashwath didn't want to enter her house, he had no choice. Naishee went down and stealthily opened the main door. She let Ashwath in. Together they tiptoed to her room careful not to wake her parents.

'Don't hate me for this.' Ashwath started the moment they entered her room.

'Softly!' Naishee turned in a trice, speaking in whispers herself. She closed the room's door behind them.

'Sorry. I've had two break-ups in college. And both times the girl betrayed me for another boy. Though they were casual affairs, their acts still hurt me. Made me feel inferior. And . . .' Ashwath said, holding Naishee's hands the moment they sat down on her bed opposite each other.

'And now you wanted to check if I was betraying you as well?' Naishee said. Ashwath pulled his hand off her and facepalmed himself.

'This isn't the time, Ashwath. My brother is missing and—'

'Trust me, this time I didn't follow you here for my own issues. You looked rattled at the apartment. I simply couldn't be at peace being in Hyderabad. So, I took a U-turn and came here. Is there any update on Shravan?'

'You could have at least told me.'

'You weren't responding to my messages too.'

Naishee rolled her eyes and preferred to give him the updates. She told him she had understood by then that if she relied on the police, it would take time. What if something bad happened to Shravan by then? For reasons unknown to her, the police didn't seem too keen on the case, from whatever she had heard about them from Mani. This was her first brush with the authorities. And surprisingly, the police turned out to be the way she had always seen them in the movies: laid-back, uninterested and lame. Was there any proof that Shravan had gone to Bengaluru of his own volition, as they were assuming on the basis of his last location shown by the phone network? In fact, it was all to the contrary. Were the police behaving this way because she and her parents weren't important enough? Naishee didn't have time for all this. She knew in her gut that her brother had not gone missing out of his own will. He would never have the courage to do so. That was what he had always lacked—bravery.

Ashwath wanted to stay back, but to avoid unnecessary explanations to her parents, she convinced him that she was all right and let him leave before dawn.

The next day, she decided to go to Shravan's school. She waited till the last bell for the day rang. As the students came out, she spotted Shravan's friends walking out in a group. There was one girl and three boys. Naishee approached them.

'Hey, akka, how are you? Long time,' said one of them on seeing her. All of them knew Naishee. They had come to her house many times with Shravan. Naishee noted that there was a happy surprise in his voice.

Isn't he concerned that Shravan is missing? Naishee wondered and said, 'Aren't you guys worried about Shravan?'

Each of the students looked at each other with guilt. *Was the happy surprise a pretence?* Naishee wondered.

'You guys know he is missing, right?'

Silence again.

'What happened? Is there something I should know?' With each second, Naishee felt the friends were bottling up something. There was a palpable tension. Naishee turned to look at the girl, Bhagyashree.

'Do you know where he is?'

'No, akka. We all had a fight with him,' Bhagyashree said. The student next to her tried to stop her but knew it was too late.

'Fight about what?'

'He told us that he was gay.'

Naishee realized there was more to it than they could stand and chit-chat about. She took them to a nearby café. As filter coffee arrived for all, Naishee took a sip, looked at each of the four students one at a time and then asked, 'Did Shravan confess he was gay or did you guys make him confess?'

No one spoke.

'Guys, please. If you don't tell me, I'll have to involve the police.' Naishee sounded as though she meant business.

'Ajith saw his mobile phone where he was having a romantic chat with a guy on Facebook,' Bhagyashree spoke. Naishee turned towards Ajith. The same boy who was the first to greet Naishee outside the school.

'I didn't snatch his phone. He gave it to me. He wanted me to hold it while he was tying his shoelaces. He received a notification which I tapped open and read some of the messages.'

'Why?'

There was no answer. Naishee understood it was pointless to moral-lecture him at the moment.

'Then what?'

'I understood it was a boy. I mean, it was obvious. I updated everyone on our WhatsApp group about it.'

'Why? Because it was a boy?'

The silence that followed told Naishee she was correct. Of all virtues, there were three major ones which were rarely taught to anyone in school: gender sensitivity, inclusion and tolerance. With every passing year, Naishee thought, people's problems were ascending. If as a society we could practise these three virtues, a lot of shit could be prevented at both an individual level as well as a communal, she pondered.

'Show me the message,' Naishee spoke up sternly.

Bhagyashree showed Naishee her phone, opening their WhatsApp group. The message Ajith was talking about was indeed in the group. It was dated a week earlier. As Naishee eyed the other messages in the group, she understood they were teasing Shravan constantly. There is a fine line between simple teasing and harassment. The thought occurred to her when she noticed Shravan had left the group soon after those messages.

'Did you guys bully him into leaving the group?'

'We were just having fun, akka,' Ajith said.

'Fun? You guys were his friends, damn it, from kindergarten. You don't make fun of such things. Whatever happened to being sensitive? Is being mean the new cool?'

'Well, I did try to talk to him after he left the group, but he neither took my call nor talked to me in school,' Bhagyashree said. As far as Naishee knew, the girl always had a soft corner for Shravan.

One of the students' mothers called in between. Naishee understood she couldn't keep them for long.

'Who was the boy with whom Shravan was chatting on Facebook?' she asked. Ajith quickly took his phone out, opened Facebook and tapped on a profile. He turned the phone towards Naishee.

Vivek Khaitan. Naishee read the name under her breath.

'We didn't know he was missing until we went to Anju ma'am's class. When Shravan didn't come there, Anju ma'am told us that his father had called to tell her that he was missing,' Bhagyashree said. Then Naishee requested the kids to reach out to her in case Shravan got in touch with them or if they got to know anything substantial about him. They promised to do so.

Once home, Naishee didn't share anything about Vivek with her parents. After dinner, she asked her parents to get some sleep. Naishee went to Shravan's room. He had lived in the house without her after Naishee had moved out for her engineering studies and later for work. But this was the first time she was living in the house without her brother. His absence was haunting. Disturbing. Defeating.

She went to his bed. It was neatly done. Shravan used to make it himself. He was particular about everything in life. His study table was also sorted. Everything was in its place. Looking at his room, it was next to impossible to say Shravan was disturbed within. If one's room was a reflection of one's personality, then Shravan's seemed to be a calm one. Naishee went to his study table and started looking for anything that was seemingly odd. Anything that was out of the ordinary. Maybe some clue that could join the dots with his going missing.

Shravan's academic books were on one side of this study table; his stationery on the other. There was a packet full of grains which he used to feed to the birds every morning, along with water, on the terrace. Her hand went to the drawers. There were three of them one below the other. She pulled out the first one that had old books; some of the books were hers, which Shravan was using. A lot of school notebooks were there. Then in the second drawer, there were some stapler pins, Fevikwik, a stapler and some paper clips. The third drawer had a small diary. Naishee had never seen the diary. She took it out, pulled out the study table chair and sat on it.

As she went through it, Naishee realized it read more like a personal diary where Shravan had made some random observations of his life since the age of eleven. There was a mention of Vivek as well in the recent entries, and that he was his first love. On the last page of the diary, he had scribbled all his social media passwords. She couldn't control her tears when she read the password of his Facebook account. *Mysismyironlady09*. The digits were her birthdate.

A little later, she logged into Shravan's Facebook account using the password. She went to Vivek's message screen and realized Vivek had deleted the messages sent by him. Only Shravan's messages were visible now. Reading them, and also the diary confession of Shravan, Naishee now was absolutely sure that Ajith was right. Vivek was Shravan's boyfriend. She thought for some time, then messaged Vivek from Shravan's profile.

Hi, how are you?

It was only in the morning when she woke up and checked whether Vivek had replied or not that she realized Vivek had actually blocked Shravan.

* * *

Chapter 6

Naishee took the bus to Bengaluru. She waited by a restaurant near the bus stop until Ashwath drove there from Hyderabad. Naishee had already called him to say she was going to Bengaluru. He'd just reached his place there when he received her message. Ashwath didn't complain. After a quick shower, he was on his way to Bengaluru. This time, Naishee was heading to the Garden City not only because she lived there but also because Vivek's current city on his Facebook profile read: Bengaluru. And according to the police, Shravan's last phone location was traced to the city. The only obvious reason that she could now think of for her brother's possible arrival in the city, if at all, had to be Vivek.

As Ashwath picked her up from the bus stop and started driving towards her rented apartment in Hosur–Sarjapur Road Layout, Naishee began going through the Facebook messages exchanged by Shravan and Vivek. She realized that if there was nothing fishy between Shravan and Vivek, the latter wouldn't have blocked him.

'But now what? Should we report this development to the police?' Ashwath asked, driving steadily. Naishee had briefed him about the development on the phone before leaving for Bengaluru herself.

'To hell with the police. Can't waste time like appa, going there every day and sitting for hours only to be told that nothing substantial has been found. Or that they think Shravan will come back when he wants to. I think we will have to meet Vivek.'

'We don't even know where he lives.'

'We can't go to him. We'll have to bring him to us.'

'How is that even possible?' Ashwath voiced what Naishee had been wondering about all through her bus journey.

They kept driving in silence. She noticed Ashwath was giving her strange glances. As if he had something in mind but wasn't sure if he should say it out loud.

'I'm listening,' Naishee said, to ease him out.

'Okay, I know this isn't the right time, but I think you should know this. My dad was asking if we should block the date for our engagement. I'm yet to tell him about Shravan's disappearance, though. I bought time saying I have an important project going on. Once I finish it, in a few months, we can decide the date.'

'Thanks, Ashwath,' Naishee said and held his hand, which was on the gearstick. She'd learnt from her previous failed relationship that one shouldn't relay what one feels about one's partner all the time. Especially the good things. It creates a perfect image of the partner about himself. And that illusion about one's own perfection dipped in male ego can become toxic. Thus, Naishee spoke little about Ashwath to Ashwath. She used to do so with her ex. She used to tell him how much she liked that he took care of her. That he was being the ideal boyfriend. That she was lucky to get him. Slowly her ex started thinking that she was lucky to have him and would be miserable without him. Things went downhill from there.

At present, somewhere she felt blessed to have Ashwath in her life. He had his issues, such as stalking her back to her place, which she didn't appreciate one bit, but the positive thing was he never probed her much. He knew when she needed space and when she needed his shoulder. That was one bit of wisdom which was rare in men. In the end, all one needs to do in order to select the person he or she wants to be with in life is to check whether the good points outweigh the bad ones or not.

'Do you have something in mind to get Vivek to us?' Ashwath asked, coming to a stop at a red traffic signal.

'I do, but I'm a little confused. But I guess I do have a solution to that confusion as well.'

By the time Naishee reached her apartment, she had made two new profiles—one with a sexy man's picture and another with a sexy woman's picture. From both, she sent friend requests to Vivek. Five hours later, when Vivek accepted the sexy woman's request, Naishee had only one question: Had he made a fool out of Shravan with his sexuality?

Though Naishee had messaged Vivek the moment he accepted the friend request, it took two days for the messaging to get going with Vivek. And he finally agreed to meet up with the fake profile woman on the upcoming Saturday.

Naishee and Ashwath reached Orion Mall before time. They had decided to meet at the Starbucks inside the mall. Vivek reached five minutes late. He'd messaged on Facebook that he would be late. The meeting happened because Vivek had audio-called Naishee on Facebook. Perhaps he was making sure there was indeed a girl on the other side. Rarely did it happen in India that a girl would ask out a guy within one week of a social media connect. Satisfied, Vivek had confirmed his availability.

When Vivek reached the mall, Ashwath, sitting right by the entrance, alerted Naishee, who was inside Starbucks, through a call from his hands-free. As Vivek came into Starbucks, he looked around. Naishee stood up, looking at him. Vivek looked at her. He seemed to recognize her. He immediately turned and dashed out.

'He moved out. Look out,' Naishee said on her hands-free. Ashwath was instantly alert. He noticed Vivek's brisk walk towards the exit and moved towards him. By the time he caught hold of him, Naishee came up behind him.

'Vivek, let's not make it difficult. I'm sure you know who I am else you wouldn't have run.'

'Easy or we are calling the police,' Ashwath said, holding Vivek tight. The latter did try to fidget but realized Ashwath was too strong for him.

Five minutes later, all three were sitting in Starbucks like civilized human beings.

'Why did you block Shravan?' Naishee asked.

'We had a bad break-up recently. He was being a pile-on. I clearly told him my gayness was a phase. And I wanted to explore women too. He couldn't take it.'

'How do I know you are telling the truth?'

Vivek shot an incredulous look at both Naishee and Ashwath.

'You can ask him. I know he must have sent you both.' Looking at Naishee, he added, 'He'd shown me your picture when we were dating.'

Ashwath wanted to explain that Shravan was missing but Naishee kicked his foot. Ashwath remained quiet. Going by what Vivek had said, it was evident that he didn't know Shravan was missing.

'When was the last time you spoke to him?' Naishee asked. Vivek opened his phone to see the last calls. He showed them his phone where an incoming call from Shravan was on the record.

'Two weeks ago,' he said.

'Did he come here to meet you?'

'Here, as in Bengaluru? No way. I never shared my address with him.'

'But he obviously knew you were in this city.'

Vivek nodded with an 'it's obvious' look on his face.

They let Vivek leave. Naishee stopped the video on her phone when she saw him leave the mall. She'd recorded the entire session.

'You think he's reliable?' Ashwath asked.

'Not sure. But right now we don't have any option. We sniff anything that brings us to Vivek, I'll involve the police.'

It made sense to Ashwath.

On the work front, Naishee had to move on with two important upcoming projects. Both were destination weddings. She travelled to Jaipur for one and then went to Goa for the second, with no break in between. Ashwath joined her in Goa on the penultimate day. By then, close to a month had gone by and they hadn't heard anything about Shravan. Not that she had given up the hope of finding her brother, but Naishee felt a part of her mind was pushing her to move on while another was shooting one question after another. Her parents too, in a way, had accepted that perhaps the police were right. That Shravan had gone away on his own accord. She had sent numerous messages to his phone but none of them had been delivered.

When Naishee went to the beach with Ashwath early in the morning, she missed Shravan the most. One of the places the siblings had planned to visit once he had passed his standard twelve exams was Goa. Sitting at the beach, staring at the waves, she asked Ashwath, 'Is life that frivolous? One day you're here and the next you are not.'

Ashwath knew it was rhetoric. Naishee didn't want a conversation. He only held her hand. They sat there in quietude. Later, he watched Naishee write Shravan's name on the sand. Then she kept looking at it with moist eyes, till the waves washed it away, one letter at a time.

Nine hours later, her flight from Goa touched down in Bengaluru. Ashwath had taken a flight back to Hyderabad from Goa. He had informed her that he would shift to Bengaluru soon, because of three reasons: First, he had resigned from his job. Second, the stand-up comedy scene was better in Bengaluru. Third, Naishee was there. In her mind, she too wanted it. Since Shravan's disappearance, she had started craving companionship more than before.

The back-to-back wedding projects in Jaipur and then Goa had exhausted Naishee. Mentally, she was anyway overworked. Getting into the cab outside Bengaluru Airport, she decided to sleep out the day. It took her two and a half hours to reach her apartment. While she was unlocking the main door of her flat, the security guard came running. He had gone to the washroom when she'd come in and had missed her.

'Madam, this had come for you.' He gave her a parcel. Naishee took it with a frown. The guard went away. She stepped inside her flat, locked the door behind her and checked the parcel. The sender's address was that of her home in Karur. Her parents didn't even know she was in Bengaluru. Who had sent this? She tore open the parcel and saw a smartphone inside. It looked like a second-hand phone. She switched it on. There was 10 per cent battery left. The phone was formatted. There were no apps. No contacts. No network. Just a nondescript wallpaper with a strange design. The only app on the front screen was the photo gallery. Naishee tapped on it. There was a video there. A single video. As she played it, her heart skipped a few beats.

She could see the camera aiming at a container of sorts on the screen. The kind found in under-construction sites. It was made to house the builder's temporary site office. There were two placards beside it. One stated an address. The other read: *I'm here, akka.*

* * *

Chapter 7

Twenty-One Years Ago

The orphan teen was one among fifty-three orphan kids who were sent to a school in Vellore, Tamil Nadu, from their sister concern in Nellore, Andhra Pradesh. The school in Nellore had closed down due to a land dispute. The trustees of the group decided to shift the students immediately to Gita Vidyashram in Vellore. The orphan teen was thirteen; the youngest in the group. While the others were admitted to their respective classes, she joined standard six. She'd come with a special letter from the principal of the sister orphanage school that she was their meritorious student.

The orphan teen had a mature figure for her age. She was made aware of it by other students in the orphanage. Their constant gaze made her keep her hands folded around her most of the time. It had gone into her head that the first thing anyone would notice about her was her breasts, though her innocence didn't let her decipher why people stared at her breasts—be they male students or guards or other men in the neighbourhood. The orphan teen had no one to share her insecurities or fears with. She was always a loner, but as she entered the new school, she became further reticent. She was not the kind who could make friends easily. Staying in the orphanage, she was socially awkward. Not that all the others were the same. Most of them gelled well in the new school scenario. Not her. Though she did learn Tamil quickly compared to other Telugu teens, she still had problems opening up.

The first day in the new school for the orphan teen also happened to be the day when the school had an inspector from the state board coming in to supervise the happenings at the school. When the inspector came to the orphan teen's class, he asked a question to the entire class in front of the history teacher, whose class was going on then.

'Where was Subhash Chandra Bose born?' the inspector asked.

Three students raised their hands. The inspector looked at one of them. The student stood up and answered, 'Calcutta.'

'Very good, Mira,' the history teacher said jubilantly. The inspector looked unimpressed. He was about to turn towards the history teacher when he heard another student speak up.

'It was Cuttack, sir.' It was the orphan teen. She had said it meekly. As she stood up, she made sure she had her hands folded around her bosom.

'Who asked you to speak? And stand straight.' The history teacher sounded rude.

'Excuse me,' the inspector spoke. 'The student is right. It was indeed Cuttack. What's with this wrong information you are teaching the kids? Shame on you.' The inspector marched off. The history teacher gave a mean look at the orphan teen and followed the inspector out.

Later that day, the history teacher was suspended for a month by the principal at the behest of the inspector, as well as for putting the school in a bad light.

That night, the history teacher sat down with his best pal, who was also a teacher at the same school, over a drink at their staff quarters and began hissing out expletives against the orphan teen. He was known to have a temper problem and had been warned many times by the school authorities after beating students severely. But this time it was different. He had been suspended. It would stay as a black spot in his career forever.

On the other hand, his best pal, who used to teach science, was a quiet person. But that was his exterior. His mind was a cesspool of perversion. He used to bully the female teachers, inappropriately touch female students and female staff, and used to fuck cheap whores on weekends, role-playing with them using the names of the teachers or sometimes even the students. His good luck was that no one had ever complained about him. That was proof of how much the women in that society were neck-deep in the mud of patriarchy, chained with the scare of shame and a bad reputation.

Listening to his friend's relentless rant against the orphan teen, he suddenly realized he had had enough. He had seen the teen himself. The way she kept her hands folded against her bosom made him wonder what would it be like to touch her bare breasts forcefully. And the way her fully formed calf muscles would give way to perfectly meaty thighs only made his dick rise up slowly. He smirked, finishing his drink. Then turned towards his friend, adjusting his lungi.

'Let's fuck her up.'

The history teacher looked at his friend. He was the only one who was well-versed with his friend's mind. Call it a heat-of-the-moment thing or the alcohol or a visceral sense of revenge against the orphan teen, the history teacher said aloud, enraged, 'Let's fuck her up.'

The orphan teen had her breakfast on time in the hostel where all the other orphans were put up. The hostels for boys and girls were separate but their school was the same. It was a ten-minute walk from the hostel to the school. As the orphan teen walked on her way, all alone, she noticed a bike slowing down beside her. She knew the person riding the bike was a teacher in the school, but she was yet to attend his class.

'*Kalai vanakkam*, sir,' the orphan teen said softly.

'Good morning. From the hostel?' the science teacher asked. The orphan teen nodded. The science teacher looked around. There was no other student in sight.

'Why are you taking the long route? Every other student takes the shorter route. It takes two minutes to reach school. Just take the left ahead and then straight. You will reach school.'

'Thank you, sir.' Though she wasn't sure whether she should take the left, she thought it was better to obey her teacher. The teacher rode off while she took the left. Fifteen minutes later, she hadn't caught sight of the school. Instead, the eerie loneliness scared her. Forgoing walking ahead, she took a U-turn hoping to return to the main road. Before she could take one step in the direction from where she had come, the orphan teen felt a strong push from behind. She collapsed to the ground. And blacked out the next instant.

When the orphan teen opened her eyes, everything was dark around her. The kind of dark one sees when one keeps one's eyes closed tight. She could feel her fear forming knots in her stomach. Even after her eyes got used to the darkness, she could see nothing and hear nothing except for the sound of torrential rain. The nature of the sound told her the ceiling wasn't made of concrete. Close to shitting her pants, she moved a little to realize even the walls weren't concrete. She understood she was in some kind of an iron container. With a shivering breath and tight fear-knots in her stomach, the orphan teen screamed her lungs out. But she knew the scream was muted by the sound of the rain. She started crying. Out of fear, she even peed in her pants. A few hours later, she heard another sound apart from the rain. She noticed the door was being opened.

The orphan teen saw a man enter, holding up a cigarette lighter. It was her history teacher. She thought he was there to rescue her. She ran towards him and held him tight. Then realized another of her teachers had also come in. The one who had suggested the shortcut to her. The science teacher.

'Sir, there was no shortcut.' The orphan teen was shuddering. Her breath was short.

'My bad,' the science teacher said.

'He told you about the shortcut, but didn't he tell you about the ghost who lurks around on this road and jumps on to young teenage girls?'

'Ghost?' The orphan teen looked as though she was about to lose her voice. She saw the teachers nodding.

'That ghost has possessed you now,' the science teacher said.

For a moment, the orphan teen thought the fear within wouldn't allow her to breathe again. That she was about to die any moment now. She could hear her own heartbeat even amidst the incessant rain.

'We will have to exorcise the ghost by taking it out from where it's hiding in your body,' the science teacher said.

'Where . . . is it hiding, sir?' the orphan teen asked, looking scarily at herself.

'Inside your underwear,' the history teacher said.

The orphan teen heard the two break into lecherous laughter. For the orphan teen, this was scarier than her stint in the container.

* * *

Chapter 8

The address in the video was of a place on the outskirts of Bengaluru. Naishee wanted to share it with Ashwath until she noticed a third, smaller placard in the video. It read: *Tell anyone and you won't find me.* Naishee had to make a decision. And she did.

When Ashwath called to check on her after reaching Hyderabad, she told him that she was going to sleep the day out. She would call him after she woke up. Ashwath understood because he too was thinking of doing the same. The call ended quickly. Naishee immediately booked an outstation Uber, dressed and took the phone she received in the parcel with her. The Uber came half an hour later. It took the cab three and a half hours to reach the location. The location had read: Sky Dream Homes. It sounded like a residential complex to her. When she reached the place, she realized she was almost right. There were a total of five buildings, all half-built. It was a no-brainer to guess it was a deserted place. There was no one in the vicinity. Not a single soul. In fact, for the last ten minutes of her drive, she had not seen or even heard anyone around. The entire vibe of the place was that of a deserted island. *What would Shravan be doing here?*

Naishee did ask the cab driver to wait, but he said he had to go back to Bengaluru since there was no network available and he wouldn't get any rides. She was the first passenger of the day for him. As the cab driver went away, Naishee realized how lonely the place was. And that the loneliness had a certain eeriness to it. She opened the video once again on the other phone. The address was the same. The container with the placards had to be nearby somewhere, she told herself.

Naishee entered the iron gate of the complex, which was ajar. Quite rusted too. It creaked open with a loud noise as Naishee pushed it to move in. With every step, she understood how spooky an empty, under-construction place could be. She observed that the buildings were half-constructed in a circular form and in the middle was an open space. The kind where builders put a children's park or a jogger's track of sorts. Naishee kept walking and reached the open space. Looking around all the while, her eyes were seeking an iron container.

'Shravan?' She raised her voice, looking around. Her echo came back. It gave her the creeps. She preferred the quiet. A few seconds of silence later, she heard a sound. As if someone was beating on some iron. Naishee's heart started racing. She began following the sound. The frequency and intensity of it rose as she started getting closer. She took a turn from the third building and noticed an iron container at some distance. It seemed to be the same one that was in the video. Except there were no placards beside it, as there were in the video. The beating of iron was coming from . . . she wasn't sure if someone was beating it from the inside or from behind it. With unsure steps, she approached the container. The sound stopped by the time she reached it. There was only one door in sight and it seemed slightly open. Naishee went to it and pushed it further open.

'Shravan?' Naishee called out with apprehension. No response. She peeped in. There was absolute darkness inside. She looked behind once, then stepped inside the container. By now she could hear her own breath, which was turning shorter with every second.

Maybe someone had kept Shravan captive inside, she thought. Naishee went in, switching her phone's flashlight on. It wasn't a big container. She couldn't locate Shravan anywhere. Halfway in, she realized it was a mistake getting inside this dark hole. It was suffocating inside. She started to sweat. Sure that Shravan wasn't inside the container, she turned to move out. The moment she did so, Naishee heard someone close the container door. As she looked at the entrance with horror, she heard the latch being drawn on the door. She dashed to the door and started banging on it with all her might.

'Hello? Who's there? Shravan? Open the door! Open the fucking door! Who's there?' Naishee kept screaming for quite some time. The only response she got was stoic silence. Her nervousness made her drop both her phones. Naishee had charged the phone she'd found in the parcel before moving out but not 100 per cent. And hers was already at 75 per cent when she had arrived here. She picked up the phones and was about to call Ashwath when she noticed there was no network. No Internet. Outside, she knew, there were no people around.

Naishee had been trapped. It was the first thought she had when no one came to her rescue even after close to one hour of relentless banging on the door. She sat down on the container's floor, with the flashlights of the phones on, drew her legs to her chest, and kept staring at the phones for a single lead of the network to appear so she could call Ashwath or her parents. Even a missed call to them would have relieved her a bit. Hours went by. She closed her eyes when the other phone went dead. A little later, her own phone's battery also died. It made the only source of light go off. There was absolute darkness even though she knew it was day outside. The darkness seemed like a monster that had surrounded her, not letting her breathe normally. The walls, too, seemed to close in on her.

She screamed her lungs out for help. Not once. Not twice. Till the last ounce of energy was left in her. Then she wept. Then went quiet. Even after forty hours of her entrapment, no one came. And Naishee thought she would die, if not out of waiting, out of hunger and thirst. Time passed on.

During the forty-ninth hour since Naishee had been trapped in the container, she heard a sound. Was it a hallucination? She wasn't sure. Then a source of light appeared. She realized it was real. Someone had opened a small gap at the other end of the container. Something had been pushed in. The opening was then closed. Naishee, who was sapped of energy by then, didn't know what exactly it was, but she managed to slowly stand up. The container's ceiling was four feet above her head. She walked up to whatever was slipped in with the support of the container walls. She bent down to feel what had been pushed in. It felt like a plate. Then she felt a polythene cover on it. She tore it apart. The scent of food invaded her nostrils. She felt a couple of soft rolls. Without caring for anything else, she gobbled them up. Tasting it, she understood they were chicken rolls. Naishee didn't stop till she had emptied the plate. She was relieved to feel a 1-litre bottle of water beside the plate. She drank half of it in one go and kept the bottle with her.

What Naishee thought was an aberration became a routine. Every day, at unpredictable times, one or the other part of the container would open and food would be pushed inside. The weird part was every time Naishee chose to sit by the spot where the opening was, the food would be pushed in from a new opening. It told her that her entrapment had been planned in advance. As time passed she had no idea about the date, day or night. She had been limited to only three basic activities: eat, sleep, excrete. She had found a corner in the container for the last. Initially it stank, but later she became used to that as well.

There were times when she started weeping without any trigger. And there were times when she felt enraged. She kicked and banged the container walls with all her might, only to feel weak and collapse on the floor.

Though Naishee had no idea how long she had been in the container, it had been a month. To begin with, existing within the container was all about fear. Would she get out? Would she die? Where was Shravan? Why did the video say Shravan was here? Did he die here? Would she too die here? After some days, she kept wondering what Ashwath must be up to. Her parents? Were they looking for her? And then came a phase where she was only thinking about old memories. When she was a kid, when Shravan and she used to fight over silly things and the like. Then a phase passed where she thought about nothing. She sat like a lump, ate when the food was given, and then sat tight again.

On the thirtieth day from the time she was entrapped in the container, the main door opened. Naishee thought she was daydreaming. She didn't move for the longest time. When the light coming in didn't go, she managed to stand up and slowly walk out of the container holding both the phones tight. As she stepped out, the sunlight hit her eyes, which made her squint immediately. She looked around. The place was the same as it was when she'd arrived there a month ago.

Naishee noticed a parcel on the ground. She picked it up, tore the envelope open and found another phone. This phone, too, was of the same model as the one she had received before, at her place. When she switched it on, as before, there was nothing in it except for the photo gallery, and in it a video. The video started with a placard that read:

Gear up, you will need to pass an exam to save your brother.

* * *

Chapter 9

Naishee moved out of the rusty iron main gate of the Sky Dream Homes site and kept walking until she reached a place where there were some shops and a few residences. Her legs were giving up by then. She did stop many times in between hoping she'd see a car or a bike for a lift. But none of it happened. Hunger and thirst made her head constantly reel. The good thing was that she had her wallet with her. The moment she started seeing people around the small shanty shops, she got her survival-will back.

Naishee went into one of the small shops and requested for some water. The *anna* sitting behind a stone desk had a big bowl in front of him and a small one beside it. From the big one, he was serving idlis to the few people around, while from the small one he was ladling coconut chutney on small banana leaves he had heaped at one corner of the stone desk.

Naishee went to him and asked for five plates of idli. He looked up at her. The last time she had had food was twenty hours earlier. The smell of the chutney made her gut further crave food. Only after finishing those five plates and then gulping some water from the common water jug placed there, did she feel alive.

Naishee looked around registering the faces of the people beside her for the first time. Most of the people there seemed to be labourers. She was the only female among them. She conversed with a few in Tamil and learnt that a couple of them had worked in Sky Dream Homes, but the project had stopped two years ago due to some funding issue with the builder. No one had gone there since. Next, she asked the anna for some directions. Following his directions, after a good two-kilometre walk, she ended up at a place that seemed populated with people. There were small but better houses and bigger shops. She headed to one of the shops and requested a phone charger.

She waited until her phone was 100 per cent charged. Then she switched it on. She was appalled to see the date. A month had passed by. There was a barrage of messages. That was obvious and expected. Most of them were from Ashwath. Some were from her workmates. She ignored the work messages. Naishee messaged Ashwath saying she was all right and would be reaching her apartment but asked him not to call her right then. Naishee needed some time to process whatever had happened in the last thirty days before blurting out to someone else about it. The placard stating 'Gear up . . .' wasn't the only thing in the video that was sent to her in the parcel. There was more. But that was for later. Naishee booked an Uber. It arrived in forty minutes.

Sitting in the car and wondering about what had happened in the last month, Naishee caught a glimpse of herself in the rear-view mirror above the driver. This was the first time in one month she had seen herself. Her eyes looked withdrawn, her jawline was more pronounced in a famished manner, her hair was unbelievably dry and she'd lost quite some weight. *What was the point of all this? Had Shravan come home because of the torture she had undergone?* She wouldn't complain if that was the case. But she doubted her brother would be home, because of the content on the other video she had received. All Naishee could conclude at that point in time, after watching the video on the phone, was that someone was playing a sadistic game with Shravan and her.

She swallowed a lump wondering where all this was leading to and looked out of the window, taking in some fresh air after a long time. She didn't dare look at herself in the mirror again during the drive.

Naishee had shared her live location on WhatsApp, so Ashwath was there by the main gate when she arrived in the cab. As he hugged her tight, both had tears in their eyes.

'What happened to you? Where the hell were you?' Ashwath asked, not ready to break the hug.

Naishee knew if she talked then, she would break down. She took a deep breath, a grip on herself and felt steadier.

'Later. Any news of Shravan?' Naishee whispered in his ears.

Ashwath broke the hug, looked deep into her eyes and said, 'Nothing.'

He held her hand as they walked to the apartment. As they stood by the elevator, Ashwath informed her that her parents were inside. That they were there since two days after she went off the radar. He had to tell them that she lived in Bengaluru.

'I didn't tell them about the photography and all,' he said. As the elevator doors closed, they began kissing impetuously. There was great hunger in both of them. They stopped only when the elevator door opened. Both her parents were right outside. She hugged her mother, then her father. Looking at her, both knew that everything was not fine.

As they entered the flat, Naishee noticed a policeman sitting on the couch finishing his tea.

'Hello, Naishee. We have been looking all over for you.' His voice was deep and on the verge of being threatening. 'Care to tell us what happened with you in the last month?'

In the hour that followed, it didn't matter how straight or roundabout a manner officer K. Bharath tried to squeeze out information from her, but she stood by what she had said to begin with.

'I was just done with the trauma of Shravan's disappearance. I took a break without telling anyone. I know it put everyone in a fix but I'm sorry, I couldn't help it.'

The officer finally stood up, unconvinced of Naishee's statement but knowing he couldn't do anything more about it. Her father escorted him to the elevator.

'Mr Kamaraj, I know your daughter is lying to me. I don't know why, though. And if she doesn't want to file a case, I can't push her to. But if you get to know anything and wish to take the police's help, do reach out to me. You already have my number.'

'Sure, sir. I will,' Mani said. As the officer went away in the elevator, Mani went inside the flat.

'Naishee, why are you lying? Where the hell were you? Is it related to Shravan?' he asked.

'No, appa. It's not related to anyone.' Naishee stood up and went to the washroom. Ashwath sat there clueless. She did hear her father and mother engage in some twaddle where he was complaining about how she had kept them in the dark about her Bengaluru stay, how her appearance was speaking volumes that she was hiding something, while her mother asked him to be happy their daughter had returned almost unhurt. Naishee heard all that but she couldn't have cared less. She locked the bathroom door, stripped herself to her skin and stood under the shower. As she sensed water on her parched skin after a month, she felt as though she wasn't a body any more but only a soul. She felt light and to an extent, relieved. Then she started crying, not believing that she had come out alive from the horror she had been subjected to for thirty days and nights straight. *Her fault? She was Shravan's sister? This can't be it or was it?* she wondered.

When everyone sat in the hall after lunch, her parents wanted to stay back, but Naishee didn't want them to. She booked their bus ticket back to Karur.

'We are concerned about you,' Meenakshi said.

'Leave it. She won't understand what concern is. Else she wouldn't have lied about being in Bengaluru!' Mani lamented.

Naishee remained quiet. She didn't have the emotional or physical energy to debate with her father about something that was already done. She had resigned from Deloitte a couple of years ago. This they didn't know yet. Ashwath had kept quiet about it the entire time. He felt good that he didn't tell her parents about her resignation, or else it would have been tougher for Naishee. It anyway was a family matter which Ashwath didn't want to get into. Naishee too was thankful that he didn't indulge in the discussion. When Mani and Meenakshi left in the evening for the bus stop, Naishee sat on the hall couch with some relief. It was then that Ashwath came to her, clasped her hand and said, 'Now tell me.'

Ashwath couldn't understand what disturbed him more. Naishee's story—what happened to her—or the fact that she was crying uncontrollably while talking. He had never seen her crying or helpless like this before. For him, she was the strong woman from whom he had drawn inspiration in his life. And took the bravest step in his own life. He wasn't just in love with her, but in some ways, he was in awe of her courage as well. He gently kissed her cheeks and wiped her tears when she was done talking.

'I would suggest, perhaps, we should accept that Shravan won't come back. I know it's—'

'There's something more,' Naishee cut Ashwath off. She went to her bedroom where she had kept her bag. Ashwath followed her inside. And saw her take out a parcel from the bag.

She opened the second parcel that she had found outside the container. She opened the video in it to show it to Ashwath.

He saw the placard first, which asked Naishee to gear up for an exam to save her brother. Then another placard asked her to check for an exam paper. Naishee took it out of the parcel and gave it to Ashwath. He paused the video and checked it. The paper had LIFE EXAM written at the top. And below there was a question. Naishee unpaused the video. Ashwath read yet another placard on it which said: *The full marks for the exam are 100. This question is for twenty marks. You will have to score more than fifteen with your answer if you want to pass and get to the next question. And your total marks should be more than seventy to save Shravan.*

They couldn't see who was changing the placard when it changed for the fourth time in the video. *Write your answer on the sheet, take a picture and mail it to*—an email ID was given. *You have twenty-four hours. If not answered then . . .* The placard was removed and in came the visual of Shravan. His eyes were open. He looked scared. His mouth was stuffed with a gag and his limbs were tied. He was lying on the ground which seemed to be dug around him. Some earth appeared on the frame and then fell on his feet and calves, burying them. The video ended exactly then. The implication was simple. Whether Shravan would live or the earth would engulf him alive would depend on Naishee's progression of the exam.

'Come on, this is bullshit. Who does this?'

'Some psychopath?' Naishee said. Ashwath's train of thought stopped. She had a point. There was silence.

'The question that I need to answer is,' Naishee took the sheet from Ashwath and read out loud, 'What did you learn staying inside the container for thirty days?' There was some space for her to write her answer. Naishee was already lost in thought. So was Ashwath. But for a different reason. He was in two minds whether he should tell her that the email ID given to her, which she was supposed to mail her answer to, was once used by him, years ago.

* * *

Chapter 10

At the age of forty-six, Muthu was a virgin. He had never married and now he had given up hope. He lived a pretty basic life in one of the corners of Karur. The house he lived in was built by his father while the small grocery shop on the ground floor had been opened by him.

The space behind the house was a lonely one with a pond right beside it. It was mostly full of rubbish. But it was also an area for young, unmarried couples to come and spend some intimate time. It was mainly due to this reason that Muthu had ordered a camera and fixed it atop his house facing the pond area. He had hidden it by placing some plants around it. No one from downstairs would be able to spot it. He wasn't afraid of any thieves for he knew they wouldn't get anything worthwhile from his place or shop. He had put the camera up to relieve himself at night. Muthu used to climb up to his home at night after closing the shop around dinner time. He'd finish his food and then sit with a bottle of beer, checking out the footage. Invariably during the day, a couple or two would come there and get intimate. Most of the girls were from his locality. And his thrill was to see them getting intimate with their boyfriends.

That night when Muthu was ready, holding his hard-on after gulping half of the beer, his eyes went to something else in the frame apart from the couple who were in the foreground smooching. It was a person walking in the background, along the lines of a broken road, who disappeared suddenly. At first, Muthu thought he had drunk too much. Then he was sure his camera had captured some paranormal activity. After watching it several times, he realized the person must have fallen into the manhole there. And he seemed to have recognized the person. A teenage boy.

Meanwhile, in Bengaluru, Naishee was sitting by her apartment's window sipping steaming black coffee. Her palate had gone for a toss having water and chicken rolls for a straight thirty days. Some post-traumatic stress was still troubling her, but there was no time to connect to a shrink. Her gut told her this was only the beginning. Life had brought her to an edge and that too so fast that she didn't know what exactly to think. What had happened seemed that perhaps Ashwath was right, someone was indeed bullshitting her. *What's this exam and all?* Naishee asked herself. How can hurting, injuring and playing with someone's life be a sport for anyone? Doesn't the person know that when you play with an individual's life—in her case, Shravan's—you're also playing with his family? Or maybe that's the intention? Myriad thoughts kept gushing into her mind. Is some psycho or sociopath behind it all? They usually don't have any direct agenda. Perhaps Shravan was a victim of being in the wrong place at the wrong time.

Ashwath, who was staying back with her, had gone to receive their Zomato order from the door. He took it, went to the kitchen and brought out the mutton kebabs on a plate with some green chutney.

Naishee took a bite of the luscious mutton piece. Her face told Ashwath she was relishing good food for the first time in her life, it seemed. A half-smile touched his face.

'Is it good?' he asked.

What did you learn staying inside the container for thirty days? Naishee read the question in her mind a few times. She thought about it for a bit. There wasn't a lot of space. She had to be precise and also hope it struck a chord with whoever was going to mark her on it using whatever parameters. She had to score fifteen out of twenty, she remembered. Naishee started writing.

I don't want to write an essay here. But two things that would stay with me forever after living in that shit hole for a month are:

1. *You tortured me for no fault of mine. In fact, torture is a mild word. I understood people can harm other innocent ones because of their own demons.*

2. *Now I know I can still live without a lot of things. The ones I earlier thought were essential to my existence don't really make the cut any more.*

She took a picture of the page and opened her Gmail app. She attached the picture and typed the email ID.

'I'm mailing the answer now,' she said. Ashwath was caught unawares. *Was this the time he was waiting for subconsciously to tell her the truth about the email ID?*

'One sec,' he said.

He came to her, read her answer and then looked at her.

'That email ID was used by me years ago.'

'What?' Naishee frowned. 'When did you last use it?'

'I don't remember. Maybe in college. I thought it must have been closed. I don't remember the password.'

'Security question? So we can reset the password?' Naishee asked. Ashwath shook his head in the negative. He didn't remember it.

'But I have another solution. You send the email first,' Ashwath said.

Naishee sent the email. Ashwath tapped on her phone for some time and then gave his phone to her. Naishee took it with a frown. She noticed a WhatsApp chat.

'Your ex?' she asked.

'Hell, no. A college friend. She was a topper in all of Tamil Nadu at her graduation. Now she is an ethical hacker. I got in touch with her the moment I learnt the email address given to you was used by me once. I just coerced her into helping us with where the email ID would be accessed.'

'Brilliant! And thanks.' Naishee raised her voice. And realized she shouldn't have since her parents were asleep.

'By when can she tell us that?' Naishee asked.

'She needs a day. Assuming the email is read by then.'

'Oh, it will be. If someone went to the extent of first keeping Shravan captive, then having me in the container only to answer his question, he must be waiting for this. The only thing I'm wondering is if using your email ID has anything to do with all this. Like, is it some clue?'

Ashwath shrugged.

Naishee was correct. The email was accessed the next morning and by afternoon, Ashwath's friend told them that it was done at a school in Vellore, Gita Vidyashram.

***

Chapter 11

Twenty-One Years Ago

The orphan teen became more reticent after the container incident. She became scared of little things around her. A particular thought, that everyone was out to harm her, first nested in her mind. And then the thought became an intense feeling in her gut. The fear turned palpable every time she was alone in her hostel room. And sometimes when people were around her too. Any physical touch gave her cold sweats. Even without her knowledge, a negative emotional attunement was brewing in her. Her performance in academics declined. She had come to Gita Vidyashram as a topper; now she barely passed her exams. Especially history and science. She felt spasms in her stomach at night but there was nobody she could relay this to. Though she was thirteen, she realized there was a new problem happening with her. She started wetting the bed at night. Something she didn't remember experiencing before. Ashamed of it and scared that others would taunt her, the orphan teen used to wash the bedsheet herself in the wee hours of the night.

One day, a few months later, she heard a buzz in the hostel. Two or three girls of her age had had their first menses. Once the painful ordeal was over, they started telling other girls what to expect when it would be their turn for nature to transform them. Everyone in the hostel, one by one, had their menses, except for the orphan teen. She didn't know why. Later in the year, a time came when, just to be a part of the herd, she too used to take the sanitary napkins supplied to the hostel by the warden and behave as if she too had had her menses regularly. She had understood that society was such that anything odd would make you a laughing stock. There was no inclusivity. Being virtuous was more lip service than action.

In school, she used to be always on the radar of the history and science teachers. They used to hover around her all the time, in the class, in the school, and sometimes around the hostel as well. To begin with, she was scared of them. The ghost they exorcised from within her had made her bleed immensely. She had to take a part of their body inside her for it and she had loathed every second of it. It wasn't the only time when the two teachers had exorcised the ghost out of her. The orphan teen had become a sport for the history and science teachers. They had the vagaries of life disturbing them in their personal space and she became their only stress-buster in a wicked, dirty, sadistic and demeaning manner.

When the orphan teen couldn't take it that her menses weren't coming, she approached the science teacher after he started teaching them chapters from basic human biology. Call it borderline Stockholm syndrome, the orphan teen thought that if they could exorcise the ghost from within her, perhaps they could help with her menses as well.

'Sir, I'm not having my period like the other girls,' she said. The science teacher made a grim face as if thinking hard.

'That's a bad thing, dear,' he said. 'Let me talk to the history sir once and let you know the reason behind it.'

The orphan teen nodded innocently and walked away. She felt relaxed that at least she could talk to someone about it. After all, the teachers had helped her get rid of the ghost and it didn't matter how painful the process was.

The next day while walking to her school, the science teacher on his bike stopped her. She saw that the history teacher was on his pillion.

'We now know why you aren't getting your period like other girls your age,' the science teacher said.

'Why, sir?' she asked meekly, already expecting a scary answer.

The history teacher got down from the pillion and came close to her. In a whisper, he said, 'It's a secret. You have to keep it to yourself. Can you promise?'

'I promise, sir,' she blurted out instantly.

The history teacher threw a confirmatory glance at the science teacher and turning towards the orphan teen again, said, 'Girls have menses because they are sexually active. Else they don't.'

She didn't understand what he meant. The science teacher chose to clarify.

'It's similar to the way we exorcised the ghost from within you that night. That needs to be repeated. Every girl here has been continuously exorcised. But no one talks about it.'

The girl thought for a moment and then asked, 'Why do only girls need to be exorcised?'

'Else men won't survive,' the history teacher said and laughed out in a lewd way. She noticed the science teacher joining him in laughing at the same tempo, sharing a high five.

'We will pick you up from the hostel tonight. Be ready.' They drove off.

59

Bribing the hostel warden with some beer bottles was enough for the drunkard woman to let the orphan teen leave with them, without any official record.

The two teachers took the orphan teen to their staff quarters. The next day she bled again. It was because of the rupture of internal tissue, but she thought she was indeed having her menses. From that night onwards it became a routine—sometimes weekly, sometimes monthly—for the orphan teen to accompany the teachers to their staff quarters at night. There was no one to tell her that the psychological trauma her subconscious had suffered since the container incident wouldn't let her body undergo menses in a natural manner. This dastardly act by the two teachers went on for two years. Nobody ever saw her going in or coming out of the hostel. Nobody would have cared to inquire even if they had. To the world, they were helping orphan kids. For the staff and the system, it was animal husbandry of a sort.

Three years later, the orphan teen, now sixteen, started feeling weak one day. She started throwing up in the school canteen. She'd been feeling sick for a few days. Though her natural menses had occurred by then, however irregular, she'd missed them that month. When the science teacher saw her throwing up for three days in a row during recess, he became alert. He cornered her after school while she was walking back to the hostel and asked her some basic questions.

Did you miss your period?

Do you feel nauseous all the time?

When did you get your last period?

The answer to the last date made him do a quick calculation. Right after school, he had a talk with the history teacher and both took her to a doctor. Their hunch was right. The orphan teen was pregnant. The doctor should have called the police as she was still a minor, but that was not to be because the doctor himself was a local quack. He suggested she should undergo an abortion immediately. It seemed correct to both teachers. Unleashing their sadistic games on the orphan teen was one thing, planting a baby in her was another. They weren't ready for it. There could be legal consequences if a third person got a whiff of it.

'There's some serious illness that you are suffering from. You need to be operated on,' the science teacher told the orphan teen.

'I'll live, right, sir?' She sounded shell-shocked and shit-scared.

'Of course. But the operation has to be done today. In fact, now!'

As the quack and an equally inexperienced assistant of his started making arrangements after being given some cash from the two beasts, the orphan teen kept praying that she would live. They did administer anaesthesia but didn't realize it hadn't been done properly. She was half awake while the abortion was going on. In between, she felt acute pain on the OT table itself, screamed her lungs out and then fell unconscious. The quack thought she had collapsed. Without checking her heartbeat, he took a call on her pulse rate that she was dying. He somehow managed to abort the infant and clean her up, but even his hands were shaking. He had initially told the two paedophiles who brought her there that he had done a lot of abortions before but that was only to negotiate more cash from them. The truth was he had never opened a girl's vagina before.

The dead body of a teenage girl was the kind of scandal that the teachers couldn't afford. If caught, they could be jailed for a lifetime. For the first time in all these years, it was their turn to be scared. They beat up the quack and his assistant for performing the abortion so carelessly. They warned him to keep his lips sealed else they would report his illegal clinic to the police, and then left the place with the unconscious orphan teen.

They fled to a nearby forest on the science teacher's bike with the orphan teen wrapped in a bedsheet. By the time they reached there, they had planned to bury the orphan teen. The history teacher was dropped at his place so he could borrow a shovel from one of his neighbours. He told the neighbour that he needed it for something at the school.

He later joined the science teacher in the forest, who by then had chosen a spot to bury the teen. The history teacher started digging the earth and they took turns at it. They lifted the orphan teen, dumped her in the hole and started putting the earth back on her. Only when she was covered till her bosom did the orphan teen feel some sensation.

'Sir, sir . . . please help,' the orphan teen's weak voice was heard. Both the history and the science teachers were taken aback for a moment. Then they glanced at each other as if wondering whether they should let her live or bury her . . . alive.

* * *

Chapter 12

Ashwath and Naishee reached Gita Vidyashram in Vellore the day after. They had taken a train. From the outside, it looked like an old school structure but once they went in, the infrastructure seemed up-to-date. They had to lie to the security guard that they were from the media and had to talk to the principal as they were doing a piece on the best schools in Vellore. The guard went to check and then came back to guide them to the principal's office.

The administrative building was different from the building where the students were seated. Naishee saw some of them curiously peeping out of the windows. The school's gate didn't give the impression that a reasonably big campus was located within. Before entering the administrative building, Naishee's eyes caught sight of another building that had STAFF QUARTERS written on it in pale red iron letters.

The school principal—I.S. Krishnan—had put on his tie when he heard that media people were coming. Otherwise, he wore his tie only during the morning assembly. He stood up seeing them by the door. He looked uncomfortable with his tie on.

'Welcome to Gita Vidyashram. Please be seated. I'm sorry, which media channel are you from?' Krishnan sat down once Naishee and Ashwath took their seats opposite him.

'I'm sorry, sir, but we aren't from the media,' Naishee said. Krishnan's face fell. Then a frown appeared.

'Then who are you guys?' he asked, looking alarmed.

Naishee took a few minutes to introduce Ashwath and herself and then went on to explain what had brought them there.

'It sounds like a police matter, Miss Naishee,' Krishnan said, loosening his tie.

'It indeed is a police matter, I won't lie about that. But they haven't been as active as we want them to be. Hence, we did our bit and now the search has brought us here.'

Krishnan removed his tie now, along with his spectacles, kept them on the table and gulped down some water from the glass beside him. Ashwath chose to keep quiet and let Naishee do the talking. He had learnt from experience that there were certain times when it was better if the woman did the talking. Especially when the matter was directly related to her family.

'But I don't get it, how can I help you in any way? Your brother Shravan wasn't even a student of this school.'

'To be honest, sir, when Ashwath helped me track the IP of the person who accessed the email, I didn't know what I was seeking. Perhaps the person who took my younger brother. Perhaps my brother himself.'

She noticed a semblance of impatience in Krishnan as he glanced at his wristwatch. A classic gesture to imply 'I-don't-have-time-for-this'.

'Could you please allow us to ask the students and the staff if anyone has seen Shravan? I'm pleading with you.'

Krishnan was known as a taskmaster to all his subordinates, but only he knew how emotions got the better of him.

Krishnan made sure the students came into the assembly area before they were allowed to leave for the day. The assembly used to take place in the open space adjacent to the school building. There was a huge gathering of students from all classes right after their last period. Naishee and Ashwath stood behind Krishnan as he spoke on a microphone.

'Dear students, I'll need five minutes of yours before you leave for your homes. Here's Miss Naishee Kamaraj. She wants to talk to you all. Please listen attentively. The matter is serious,' Krishnan stepped back and gestured to Naishee to come forward. She held the mic stand with both her hands as she spoke.

'I have never done this before. So I will keep it short. My brother, Shravan Kamaraj, is missing. He didn't study here but I have some evidence to believe he may have been around. This is his picture.' As she turned, the big projector screen behind her showed Shravan's picture, which she had shared with Krishnan's team.

'If any of you, that includes the teachers and staff, have seen him around, please let me know.'

There was a haunting silence. Hoping against hope, Naishee kept looking around at the faces of the students, of the teachers, of the guards standing at the back. Everyone saw the picture; no one came forward.

Before leaving Gita Vidyashram, Naishee left her phone number with Krishnan, requesting him to reach out to her in case anyone from the school got any information. And she promised him that the school's or his name wouldn't feature anywhere.

The two were waiting at the Vellore railway station for their train back to Bengaluru.

'It was a waste of time coming here,' Naishee said. She seemed distant.

'Nothing is a waste. We had to do this. It was important. The person who kidnapped Shravan and then saw his photograph obviously wouldn't come out in the open,' Ashwath said.

Naishee glanced at him. He shrugged inquiringly. She nodded. Naishee loved the way he never spoke negatively about any action of hers. The only good thing that had happened to her in the recent past was him. She'd found someone with whom she could explore the possibility of settling down. A year ago even that possibility seemed like a joke to her. She held his arm and rested her head on his shoulder. There was this vibe of solace around him. Being with him, Naishee had understood that the person who can make your search his own, could never steer the relationship in the wrong direction. It was about each of them giving the other's issues priority. Growing beyond being selfish or self-centred. *Perhaps true love,* Naishee pondered, *is about hand-holding someone and making the person grow beyond these self-focused traits.*

Ashwath's phone rang. Naishee glanced at the phone's screen to see it was his father calling. He excused himself and went a few steps away to talk to him. He always did that. Ashwath never talked to his parents in front of Naishee. She never asked why. She kept looking at him as he talked. He seemed perturbed. After he ended the call, he came to her.

'Let's go to my place,' he said.

'Your place, as in? Chennai?' Naishee wasn't expecting this. Ashwath nodded.

'Appa is calling me there. Something important has come up. It's better we both go.'

'Did he say I should be there too?'

'No. He doesn't know we are here.'

Which was the catchword—we or here? Naishee wondered.

'Does he know we are travelling together?' she asked. Ashwath was quiet. By now Naishee had understood a trait of Ashwath. He never lied. Either he told the truth or he avoided telling a lie. But he had never told her a lie before.

66

'Your father has called you. I think you should go. I'll wait for you in Bengaluru anyway. Also, it's just a suggestion, but I think you should inform them about Shravan's disappearance.'

'Hmm. But I think we should . . .'

Ashwath did try to debate it but in the end, Naishee convinced him to take the train to Chennai alone, which was already waiting to depart on the parallel track. Without caring to book a ticket, Ashwath hopped in. When Naishee's train to Bengaluru arrived a couple of hours later, she boarded that.

Ashwath's house was in Kotturpuram, Chennai. From the time he arrived, his parents saw that he was fidgety. He always did this when he was uncomfortable about something.

'How come you came so quickly?' Dushyant Nair, his father, asked.

'If he comes early, it's a problem, and if he doesn't visit, you're still upset,' Remya, his mother, said, keeping three glasses of filter coffee on the centre table of their hall room. Ashwath took his coffee and went inside his room. His parents exchanged surprised looks.

A few minutes later, Dushyant came to his room with some photographs. Ashwath understood why he had called him home urgently. Without even a preamble, he started showing Ashwath pictures of various girls. The same drill he had done when he had shown Naishee's picture as well.

What Ashwath hadn't told Naishee was that he had already told his parents about Shravan's disappearance as well as her going missing for a month. He didn't expect his parents to take a complete U-turn based on this information. After hearing what was going on in Naishee's family, they decided to get their only child married into some other family. Ashwath knew about it but hadn't informed Naishee.

'Appa, I'm in love with Naishee. I've told you this several times before on the phone. And, it's her brother who is missing. How is she or her family responsible?'

'Shut up, Ashwath. We can't marry you off to a family where the brother is missing. Then the daughter goes missing for a month with no news of where she was. Maybe she is on drugs, god knows.'

'Not only god, even I know she wasn't on drugs,' Ashwath shot back.

'Yeah? Then where was she? What was she doing? Tell me.'

'Oh, come on, Appa,' he raised his pitch. 'She isn't on drugs. That I can vouch for. You don't have to know everything.' Ashwath stood up while speaking. His stance was confrontational. Something he had never assumed in front of his father before.

Dushyant turned to notice Remya standing by the door. He was fuming.

'Ashwath's amma, now you know why I was worked up. Your boy is already under that girl's spell.' He turned to Ashwath, 'I'm giving you a month to wrap up whatever you are having with the girl. I'm more than sure I'm not letting you marry her. No girl whose character can't be confirmed will ever become a Nair daughter-in-law.'

Dushyant dashed out of the room. Remya stood helpless where she was. Ashwath was breathing hard. Frustration was taking the shape of anger. He punched his study table forcefully. It made his mother's heart skip a beat.

'Leave me alone, amma,' he hissed.

When Naishee called him at night, Ashwath informed her he would be coming over to Bengaluru the next day itself.

'But why did your appa call you so urgently?' she asked.

'Leave it. Anything from the kidnapper yet? It's been some time since you answered the goddamn question.'

'Nothing yet. Even I'm waiting. Can't focus on anything else.'

'I get it. Tell me, have you had your dinner?'

'I did. After coming back, I realized so much work had piled up. Life has been weird in the last two months.'

'I thought they would simply announce you absconding from your company.'

'Well, they almost did. But I think someone from the office did get in touch with appa since they had his number. He told them that I had also gone, just like my brother went missing.'

Ashwath understood that she was choked emotionally by the time the last part came out.

'Just listen to me carefully. There comes a point when you have to accept the truth,' Ashwath said.

'What's the truth, Ashwath?' Now he was sure she was crying.

'Maybe,' Ashwath's throat dried up as he spoke, 'Shravan won't come back.' He instantly felt bad that those words had to come from him.

'I would have accepted it if some asshole out there hadn't sent me those videos and made me undergo the shit that he has. I'm dead sure Shravan is alive. But I can't get to him at my will. That's what the problem is.'

'And we can't share this with anybody. Not even the police.'

'Exactly. I'm convinced it's not a random kidnapping. It's a thought-out . . .' Naishee chose her words after a thoughtful pause, 'game of sorts.'

A silence took over. They ended the call with soft kisses and went to sleep.

At around 5.30 a.m., the doorbell woke Naishee up. With sleep-heavy eyes, instead of getting up, she simply tossed on the bed and was about to go back to sleep when the doorbell rang a few more times. It irked her. She got out of bed thinking, *How many times have I told the milkman to put the pouch outside and not ring the bell?* She opened the door. There was one pouch of milk, which she picked up. Naishee's sleep disappeared from her eyes as she realized the pouch had no milk; it had a mobile phone instead.

The same model that she had received before.

* * *

Chapter 13

Leaving the door open, Naishee ran downstairs. She came out of the building. There was no one around. She brisk-walked to the security guard's room beside the main gate. He was asleep. His phone was playing a local song out loud.

'Anna! Anna!' Naishee called out to him from outside the guard's small room. There was no response. She went inside and shook him vigorously. The guard woke up with a start.

'Yes, ma'am.' He stood up.

'Someone came to my flat a few minutes ago. Did you see anyone?' Naishee knew the answer but still asked.

'Sorry ma'am, I was sleeping,' he said with a crestfallen face.

A flustered Naishee looked up at the CCTV camera.

'Take me to the control room. I want to—'

'Those don't work, ma'am,' the guard said, realizing what she had in mind.

'What? Why? Since when?' She had her hands on her hips in exasperation.

'Been a week now, ma'am. We'd repaired it but it went kaput again.' The guard shamelessly blocked a yawn while speaking.

Naishee let out a defeatist sigh and walked right back to her building. She climbed the stairs and entered her flat. The milk pouch with the phone inside was lying where she had left it. Naishee picked it up, took out the phone and switched it on.

As usual, it had no apps, only a bland wallpaper with a weird design, like before. She didn't waste time getting to the photo gallery. This time she noticed a video along with pictures of some placards with text. She went through the text first; one by one.

Your score was 17/20, the first one read.

Every time a placard appeared, Naishee paused the video to read it properly. As she played the video after reading the first placard, the second one appeared on the screen.

But two marks were deducted for acting smart and going to Gita Vidyashram, read the other.

Pause. Play.

So, you have got 15 out of 20. Now for the next question.

Pause. Play.

When is your next fertile date? Full marks are 25. You get zero, if wrong.

Pause. Play.

Send your answer with proof.

Pause.

There were no more placards. Naishee tapped the play icon on the video again. It showed Shravan—more earth was being put on him. In the last video, his feet were covered. Now he was buried in earth till his knees. He looked helpless and weak as he kept staring at the camera pleadingly with moist eyes. It seemed he too didn't have any clue of what was going on. Naishee couldn't bear to see Shravan that way. The video ended. She transferred the video to her phone via Bluetooth, and then kept the phone, along with the other phones given to her, safely in her wardrobe.

Where this thing was going, she had no idea. Earlier, Naishee thought that after surviving the container and answering the question, at least she would get to hear Shravan. But all she got was to helplessly watch more earth being poured on to him. This entire unpredictable series of events had put her heart on the edge, for sure. There was not one moment when she could think of anything else. It meant the kidnapper indeed had questions that would add up to 100 as the video had stated earlier. What if she scored what was required, would it take her to Shravan? What would be the kidnapper's takeaway then? Just the thrill of tormenting innocent people? *What has this world come to?* Naishee wondered.

While sitting by the window of her flat later that day, she read Ashwath's message: *Reaching in 40 mins.*

All the phones that she had received were lying in front of her now. She not only checked their content again and again but also their make, just in case she'd missed any vital information before. She discovered nothing new. When it came to Shravan's disappearance, Naishee didn't know where to begin and what exactly to think. Everything was so bizarre. She did Google to see if such an incident had ever happened before. Generally, people got ransom calls after kidnapping someone. And this much was clear, that Shravan had been kidnapped, kept captive and the person was now playing some sadistic games with her. Would she be able to reach Shravan at the end of it? She felt an impulse within her to report all of it to the police. Maybe the kidnapper would be caught, but would she get Shravan back alive? Naishee took a deep breath and with it, she neutralized the impulse within.

Ashwath came home and found that Naishee had her suitcase open. It was half-full.

'Where are you heading?' he asked, making himself comfortable on the study-table chair in the room.

'All good at home?' Naishee dodged the question to shoot one of her own.

'Yes. Tell me, where to now?'

The way Ashwath behaved a little dispassionately while answering her, Naishee understood that he was hiding something.

She didn't probe, though. It would be better if he came out with it when he felt comfortable, she thought, and said aloud, 'Work call. I'll have to fly to Goa soon with my team. A wedding beckons.'

'When are you flying?'

'Day after tomorrow. Why, are you coming?'

Ashwath stood up from the chair he was ensconced in and walked to Naishee. He held her from behind and rubbed his nose on her nape.

'I so wish, but I have a few stand-up acts to open,' he whispered in her ear. From the first day, his touch had made her feel secure. Made her feel life would be a sunny affair. She held his hand, managed to turn in his embrace and kissed him.

'Focus on your stand-up. Don't worry about me, I'll be back real soon.'

They kissed again. The doorbell rang.

'Us and our interruptions.'

Naishee smiled, 'Has to be the delivery boy.'

Ashwath frowned as he watched her move out of the bedroom. In a few seconds, he heard her open the main door and close it. She came back with a packet in her hand.

'What's this?' he asked.

'Ovulation kit.'

Ashwath looked scared. The last time they made out, it was without protection.

'Don't worry, I'm not pregnant. This is . . .' Naishee updated him about the milk pouch. Even Ashwath seemed as clueless as Naishee about the dangerous game-like endeavour.

'Are you sure you want to proceed with all this? It seems so twisted. I think we should involve the—'

'I don't have an option, Ash. I want my brother alive. And this is the best way to make that happen. At least for the time being.'

Ashwath took the kit from her hand and examined it.

'How does this goddamn thing work?' he asked.

The ovulation kit worked in a simple manner, Naishee explained to him. It had test strips where one had to test it against one's urine. A rise in luteinizing hormone is a hint to the ovary to release an egg. When one's levels reach a certain threshold, one can safely predict that ovulation will occur within the next twelve to thirty-six hours.

'I don't know, but I'm having a bad feeling about all this,' he said.

'Well, you aren't the only one having this feeling,' Naishee said sombrely.

That night they made soft love, without penetration, before Ashwath slept. From the time Naishee had come out of the container, she was having sleeping problems to the extent that she had made up her mind to consult a therapist. But that would happen after the Goa trip. She was thankful to DK for not firing her from her job even after going missing for a month.

Naishee's boss was a lady. Everyone called her DK. Her full name was Divya Kadni. At forty-eight, she was an inspiration to her team. The grapevine was that she had undergone a lot in life to become this fiercely independent woman who was at the top of her game now. Her wedding planning–event management company was one of the best in the country. And she was known to employ an all-women team. Not because she was a feminist but because DK believed that women managed and coordinated better than men. Going by the track record of the number of weddings and events the company had organized, no one could challenge that.

Generally, DK never used to attend a shoot unless it was a celebrity client. Seeing her at the Goa resort surprised Naishee. DK, for one, loved Naishee. Neither could forget the latter's job interview. Naishee had walked in with some amateur photographs to apply for the post of assistant photographer. When DK asked her why she had decided to leave her corporate job and become a photographer, Naishee ended up telling her story. And it told DK that there was one thing common between them. They both chose their voice over what others wanted of them.

'Join us from tomorrow,' was what DK had said after the first question and perusing some of her photographs.

In no time, Naishee had been promoted to head of photography in the company based purely on her talent.

'How did you know I was any good?' Naishee had once asked her during an office party.

'Unlike others who invest in *fruits*, I invest in good quality *seeds*. And grow my own orchard,' DK had said and winked.

And now seeing her at the reception of the Goa resort, Naishee couldn't help but run to her and give her a warm hug.

'Hey girl, how have you been?' said DK, returning Naishee's hug with a momma-bear hug. DK was physically a huge woman because of some gynaecological problems.

The two chit-chatted for some time after which DK left. Naishee went to her room. Her two assistants had set up the lighting, which she went and checked before the different events at the wedding were supposed to begin. And when they did begin, there was no time to rest.

On the night of the third day, before the main wedding ceremony, she checked the ovulation kit and realized her most fertile period would be the day after, during the bride's *bidaai*—when the bride was finally sent off with the groom. She noted the time and emailed the ovulation information to the email ID. While wondering what this information could be needed for, Naishee's tired mind went to sleep. By then, she and Ashwath had concluded that perhaps it was a coincidence that the email

ID was the same as the one Ashwath had used. Old IDs did stop existing only to be taken up by someone else. It happened all the time.

The next two days were crazy. This was a destination wedding of a big fat Punjabi family who had chosen to have it in Goa. And the demands of each of the members of a Punjabi family, when it came to weddings, were at a different level, as Naishee by now had realized.

Finishing her work around 2 a.m., Naishee had a quick call with Ashwath. He was happy with his recent stand-up performances and had shared a few video clips with her where the audience had gone gaga over his opening act. She could relate to his happiness. She had experienced the same happiness herself after her first wedding event in DK's company. She remembered how happy the client was with the photographs. Self-validation was always a rich and purer source of happiness than most other things.

Drawing the curtains of her room, Naishee realized for the first time that she was actually staying in a beach-facing room. Since the time she had checked-in, Naishee had used it only for sleeping. And sometimes not even that. Her luggage had spent more time than her in the room. She quickly put on her sandals and decided to take a stroll on the beach. In the morning, she was supposed to fly back to Bengaluru with her team.

Sitting on the beach, Naishee understood why it was important to remain busy in life. Truth be told, she had not got one second to think about Shravan in the last week. And now she couldn't think of anything else. Why was her eighteen-year-old brother being subjected to such trauma? Even if he survived, if the kidnapper was to be believed, and if she passed the so-called exam, would Shravan be able to live a normal life again? Do people who are scarred this way, or in any way, remain normal?

As Naishee found herself immersing deeper and deeper into a whirlwind of questions, the orphan teen, who was a grown-up now, noticed her sitting alone from some distance away. The lurking darkness wouldn't allow either of them to see the other's face clearly even if they came close to each other. And still, the orphan lady took quiet steps towards Naishee, pressing her feet in the cold sand. One glance and Naishee would have identified her. The orphan lady couldn't take that chance. With every step, she was tightening her grip on the small iron rod in her hand.

When she reached Naishee, she simply hit her head with the iron rod from behind. No emotions exhibited. Not a fatal blow though.

* * *

Chapter 14

The orphan lady, with locked jaws, was pulling an unconscious Naishee with both hands along the sand. After seven minutes of non-stop movement, they reached a boat anchored by the beach. The orphan lady first took a breather, then put Naishee on it with some effort. Naishee's head was bleeding slightly. The orphan lady took her time to nurse Naishee's head wound first. She had practised giving the hit to the head a number of times and knew exactly the point of attack. She knew how hard to hit so as to not fracture Naishee's skull but give her a minor concussion and knock her unconscious. There was no one in the vicinity. The entire place was blanketed in a meditative silence and miles of emptiness.

The orphan lady had a waist bag tied around her. She took out a dropper-tube and a small plastic container from it. An hour ago, she had bribed three local fishermen in the area with cash in exchange for their sperm. They couldn't believe someone would pay them for this. They happily jerked their seed out in different containers, which she then mixed and put in the small container that she was carrying. She put the dropper-tube in the container and sucked out the semen. She then tugged down Naishee's night-dress trousers, then her panties and spread her legs. She held her vaginal lips apart and gently inserted the dropper-tube. Next, she released the semen into her. Dressing her up, the orphan lady left Naishee on the boat. Though many sperms had died in the container, which wasn't sterilized, her intention wasn't to make Naishee pregnant per se. Her intention was to keep her in two minds. Whether the pregnancy would happen or not. And the groundwork for that had been achieved.

It was a local coconut seller, by the beach, who found Naishee. At first, he thought she must have drunk-slept on the boat. He had seen such women before, but most of them were foreigners. This one didn't look like one. He woke her up. For a moment, opening her eyes, Naishee didn't understand what was going on. Where was she? She looked around. The beach in the morning was still vacant except for a few foreigners jogging and a few coconut sellers in the distance. She realized she was on a boat.

The man said something to her in Konkani. Naishee, without talking to him, stepped out of the boat and started walking towards the resort. She touched her head, feeling a little pain and realized that a part of her head had some cotton stuck to it. As she pressed more, the area pained more. There was also some discomfort in her vagina. She felt like peeing. She brisk-walked to reach the resort.

Naishee reached her room and immediately went to the washroom. She checked her head injury. It didn't seem too bad but there was some pain. It was clear to her that she was attacked last night. By the kidnapper? Or was it a random attack, but for what? Not able to figure out an answer, she rushed to pee but felt some discharge coming out. Naishee touched her vagina to feel something sticky. As she sat down to pee, she could feel her heart race. The last thing she remembered was sitting alone by the beach, then the blow to her head. The injury was proof of it. What had happened next? Why was there discomfort in her vagina? By the time she was done peeing, Naishee wanted to throw up. Her mind had joined the dots. Ovulation kit . . . asking for her fertile date . . . getting her unconscious . . . now a sticky vagina with some discomfort . . . *have I been inseminated?* Naishee took the jet spray and started washing her vagina as deep as possible. She looked visibly unsteady and emotionally edgy. *What more should I do? Can I do? Pills?*

Naishee picked her phone up from the bed. She had left it there last night when she'd gone to sit on the beach. She Googled to search for a chemist near her. There were a few options but none of them was open at that time. She could feel anxiety gripping her progressively. Should she tell Ashwath what had happened? Should she go to the police? Or a . . . gynaecologist?

Feeling an acute restlessness, Naishee threw herself on the bed. When her teammates came calling, she barely managed to keep herself calm and told them she would reach the airport by herself. Naishee wanted to avoid people. She wanted to keep the development under wraps. She knew that she was looking like a wreck and was in no mood to answer any questions. Even after reaching the airport separately, she chose to sit at another end of the departure section as the flight to Bengaluru was the same for her as it was for her team. Her entire body was constantly shaking. Though she could see her team from a distance, she was relieved DK wasn't travelling with them. Dodging her boss would have been impossible and DK was a legit face reader. She would know something was grossly wrong with her, the moment she saw her.

Though Naishee was constantly chatting with Ashwath, who had gone to Delhi for a stand-up performance, not for once did she dare to tell him what had happened. *What if he starts disliking me? What if I actually get pregnant and he breaks up with me?* Thoughts that didn't necessarily have a legit emotional trigger were constantly hovering in her mind. She met her team during the flight boarding process. When her assistant tried to talk to her, Naishee was curt.

'I'm trying to catch up with some sleep. Please excuse me.' She put on her eye-pad and pretended to doze off in her seat. Throughout the flight, with her eyes closed, all Naishee could imagine was what could have happened once she had been struck on her head. She had woken up on the boat but did that mean she was inseminated on the boat or . . . did someone force himself into her when she was unconscious? She shuddered at the thought. Before the tears could seep out of her eye-pad, she wiped them, tugging the eye-pad down a bit. She went to the airplane's washroom three times, only to wash her vagina. The airport chemist didn't have a morning-after pill. And most of the chemists in the city were closed since it was too early in the morning when she moved out of the airport.

She made sure she took a pill from a chemist en route from Bengaluru Airport to her apartment. As she entered her flat, Naishee noticed it was decorated with balloons. On the wall, glam papers had been cut and arranged in an order that read: *Welcome Back.* There was a bouquet with her favourite flowers and a note. Naishee locked the door behind her and picked up the note. It read: *I know Goa must have been hectic. Just a small token of love for you. Relax . . . till I come back.* Signed: *A.*

Naishee sat down on the couch with a thud, feeling many things at once. Minutes later, she went to the bathroom and washed her vagina again. When she came out, Naishee booked an appointment with her gynaecologist. She got a slot for the next morning.

At night, while talking to Ashwath on the phone, she couldn't hold back any more. Though he did ask for a video call, Naishee knew that way he would know she was being vulnerable about something. Hence, it was a simple WhatsApp audio call they were engaged in. She took a two-minute fake loo break in between their conversation, contemplating hard whether she should tell him about what she feared had happened to her. In the end, she ended up confessing only half the truth; that the ovulation kit had come with a parcel sent by the one who had Shravan captive. It was then that Ashwath said something which blew her mind.

'Don't get me wrong,' he said with a cautionary tone, 'this is just a hypothesis I'm stating because it struck me just now. I'm sorry if it hurts you but—'

Naishee's silence told him she was waiting for him to simply speak it out.

'All right, I'll just say it. What if Shravan is already dead and these videos were shot earlier? Aren't we playing into the hands of this sadistic asshole?' he asked.

This time the silence was a little too long from Naishee's end.

* * *

Chapter 15

By the time Ashwath reached Bengaluru, Naishee had not only been to the gynaecologist but had also thought about what the doctor had said, like 10,000 times. Naishee didn't tell the gynaecologist about what she thought had happened to her. She simply told her she had unprotected sex with her boyfriend on her fertile dates and was fearing she would get pregnant. While the gynaecologist gave her the contraceptive and assured her that more often than not, if one took it within seventy-two hours, the sperms would be killed, it didn't cure Naishee's anxiety. Especially when the doctor told her that nothing was 100 per cent effective once the sperms were released inside, that too during one's fertile period. It made her even more anxious.

Waiting for Ashwath at home, Naishee wondered what Ashwath had told her the night before. If Shravan was really dead. If he was, then what was the point of her being pushed into all this? First, locking her in the container was subjecting her to physical horror. Now, it was plain mental horror she was being subjected to. Was she pregnant or not? How was she supposed to focus on her life, her work, anything? Did the kidnapper know with this one act of his what was at stake for her? Then she answered herself: of course, he knew. He knew, hence he did what he did. The question was . . . why. If Ashwath was correct, then one thing she could safely conclude: this person was indeed a sociopath.

When Ashwath came home later that night from Delhi, he found a different Naishee there. Someone who looked badgered by life. She seemed to be totally sapped of energy. He feared she was sick.

'Didn't you go to the office?' he asked.

'I skipped,' she said.

Ashwath remained quiet then. He changed, freshened up, and then went to the kitchen to prepare something for both of them. He came back and saw Naishee had not moved from where she was sitting by the window. As if she was lifeless.

'What has happened to you? Do you want to share anything?' he asked after preparing some hot soup for her.

Naishee remained quiet as she had some soup first.

'Or should we go to a doctor?' he asked a minute later, totally concerned.

'I did go to a doctor. She said she can't be sure.'

'Sure of what?' Now Ashwath was tense.

'That I would get pregnant or not,' Naishee murmured. Tears welled up in her eyes. Ashwath went close to her and took her in his arms.

'What are you talking about?' Ashwath almost had his heart in his mouth.

Naishee took a few minutes to tell him what she thought must have happened to her in Goa.

'I've applied for sick leave this month. I can't focus on anything. What's my fault? I don't want to be pregnant like this, Ash. I don't want to be destroyed like this. Please save me.'

Ashwath felt he himself could cry any moment as Naishee held him tight and wept.

'It's enough now. I think we should get to the police and push them further.'

'No! What if Shravan gets killed in the process?'

'As I said, what if he is already dead? We can't play with someone's sadistic mindset. This is the limit. You have been technically raped. We have to inform the authorities otherwise—'

'How do you think your parents will react if they get to know about this?' Naishee looked into his eyes for the first time that night. Ashwath had not told her what his parents were thinking about them. That they were already against Naishee. And with such news coming out, which it was bound to if they went to the police, it would be the last nail in the coffin as far as their marriage was concerned.

Naishee interpreted his thoughtful silence correctly.

'That's your answer, Ash. We can't go to the police. Doesn't matter even if I'm innocent, a victim. It will open up further problems for us. Not till we have solid evidence against this kidnapper. Right now, I don't even know who hates me so much to make me experience this shit. And why?'

Ashwath had no response to that except to keep caressing her back, feeling insanely frustrated.

Living the next twenty-eight days was as horrific as it had been in the container, except she felt the fear was stronger than before. It was hitting her more acutely now. Its canines were deeper into her than before. It wasn't the fear of life or death as it was inside the container, but this time it was whether she would be able to absorb the shame that would come to her if she got pregnant. What would she tell her parents? Ashwath? His family? Would anyone care to even consider seeing all this from her perspective? Naishee remembered a girl from her locality in Karur who'd been seen by one of her cousins coming out of a gynaecologist's clinic once. A rumour had spread that she had

had an abortion since she was having an affair with a boy. The girl was harassed and her family was socially cornered day in and day out, till the entire family had to relocate to another city. The truth, however, was something else. Such was the blind rage of society, which had sharp claws but no empathy.

Though initially she had applied for a month-long leave, Naishee soon understood it was better to remain at work, otherwise her head would burst with thoughts. Staying alone in her flat, she felt loneliness had become a malevolent ghost tormenting her relentlessly. Only she could feel it. No one told her directly at the office but Naishee knew she was losing her grip on work for the first time since she joined the company. She could feel it during meetings when time passed by in a blur. She had to find out from her assistants later what had transpired. Sometimes she was slow to even process information. DK was quick to guess something was wrong. She called Naishee one day to her cabin after a boardroom meeting with the entire team about an upcoming event.

'What's up with you, girl? I've never seen you so quiet in meetings before. And lost!'

'Nothing, ma'am,' Naishee said sheepishly.

'Of course there's something that's bothering you. I understand if it's too personal but it's affecting your work. And that's not good. Look, doesn't matter what happens in our personal life, a real professional is a person who leaves it all behind when she comes to work.'

'I understand, ma'am. It won't happen again,' Naishee said, but the same thing happened in numerous meetings during the following week. At home, she didn't want Ashwath to realize how tense she was as it would affect his stand-up performance as well. Whenever he wrote something and performed it in front of her, she had to laugh where the lines deserved it, to keep him going. But it was difficult. Thus, she started avoiding him in a smart way. If he wanted to go out at night for a drink, she would feign a headache and sleep. She would leave earlier than usual in the morning citing office work but would sit on a bench in a park close to her office, continuously getting probed by her anxiety till it was time for office. Not that Ashwath didn't realize it. An obsessive habit she had developed after the beach attack was washing her vagina whenever she got an opportunity. It had turned into a mania in a short span of time.

Somewhere in his own mind Ashwath, too, was fighting a battle of sorts. What if Naishee actually became pregnant? He was sure he didn't want to leave her because of it. If there was one person who knew it wasn't her fault, it was him. But he also knew it didn't matter how much he would prepare himself; his parents would simply ostracize not only Naishee but him too, if he supported her.

One night when he woke up to go to the bathroom, he noticed Naishee wasn't by his side in bed. Ashwath went out and found her on the balcony. It was clear she was crying. He couldn't bear the sight. It had been close to three weeks since she had returned from Goa. It was a totally different version of her. He knew he had to do something about it. Naishee was progressively becoming someone whom he hadn't fallen in love with. His Naishee was stronger than this. His Naishee was happier than this. And never this stuck in life. And when one is in love, it is one's duty to not let the person derail from one's life.

The next day, a determined Ashwath talked to a few friends in the stand-up comic circle and got a link to an officer in Chennai's cybercrime unit. He registered a complaint there on his own accord without telling Naishee about it and shared the email ID that the kidnapper had given Naishee.

On the fifth day, an officer from the cybercrime unit called Ashwath while he was opening an act for another comedian at a club. It was only when he went backstage that he saw a missed call from an unsaved number. When he called back, the officer told him that they had nabbed the person from Gita Vidyashram who had accessed the email. That was enough to get Ashwath's adrenaline rushing. He had to wait for the show to get over, after which he skipped dinner with the senior comedians and headed to Naishee's place. He reached there an hour later. With his spare key, he opened the door and came in exclaiming, 'Naishee!'

He found her in the bedroom with bloodshot eyes.

'What happened?' Ashwath asked. He wasn't ready for this.

Naishee handed a phone to him. It was the same model she had been getting anonymously. Ashwath took it and tapped on the play button of the video that was open.

A placard in the video read: *Thanks for going to the police.* Then the video showed Shravan whose entire body was covered with earth, except his face. With his mouth stuffed with some cloth, he was visibly trying to scream out. His eyes exhibited pure horror. More earth was put on his face, burying him entirely. The video ended abruptly.

And with it, Ashwath's excitement.

* * *

Chapter 16

Twenty Years Ago

The orphan teen was surprised when she saw a cake being brought in by the history teacher to the class. At first, she thought perhaps the teacher and she shared the same birthday. Never before had her birthday been celebrated. So the sight of the cake convinced her it wasn't for her.

Birthdays were never special for her, though she had seen how important it was for students in Gita Vidyashram. The birthday student was allowed to swap the school uniform with an outfit of his or her choice. The student used to distribute sweets to everyone, which his or her parents had bought. Not every student who studied there was part of the orphanage. The birthday rules also allowed the student only half a day in school. He or she could leave after recess. None of that was ever experienced by the orphan teen. In fact, the idea of belonging, of inclusivity, of family, were all alien to her still. Whatever she knew of it was by observing other students and their parents.

Before starting the class, the history teacher placed the cake on his table, asked one student to switch off the fan and then lit the candle in the shape of the number fourteen. Everyone was wondering whose birthday it was. The teacher looked up at the orphan teen and announced loudly to the class that it was her birthday. Everyone started clapping. The orphan teen was first totally bamboozled. She thought that she was in a dream. Then she felt shy in a way she had never felt before. There was a hint of happy embarrassment too. The teacher urged her to come forward. Since the time the teachers had saved her from being buried alive, or so she was told, she started respecting them more. Both the history teacher and the science teacher told her how the quack had tried to kill her. They thought she was dead and wanted to give her a respectful burial. She started feeling protected by them ever since. Though she never asked anyone, in her mind she knew that she belonged to the girls in the orphanage who were regularly exorcised like her. It was 'normal'. She wasn't some freak who was possessed by the ghost alone. The wretched humans who were her teachers, after all, had registered themselves as heroes in her innocent mind. Their sport with her, however, continued in the same dastardly manner it had started from the container.

The orphan teen stood up and with unsure steps went in front of the class. She was given a small knife. It was the first time she had seen a birthday cake with her name written on it. She blew out the candle and cut the cake as everyone in the classroom clapped. The teacher cut out one piece and let her have it. Then, he cut the cake into small, equal pieces and asked the class monitor to distribute it to the students. The orphan teen went back to her seat feeling an absolute kind of happiness for the first time in her life. She could sniff love in the way the students clapped for her. A belief invaded her that even she could be the centre of attention. That her birth perhaps had some importance if not a purpose yet.

That night in her hostel, the news of her birthday had spread to everyone. The seniors gave her birthday bumps. She took it happily. The hostel, for the first time, didn't look like a morose, sombre refugee camp of sorts where no one was her pal. She thanked everyone and went to bed. This was the first time she had talked to them one-on-one. Otherwise, she was always the wallflower in the group.

She lay on her bed still, with her hopeful eyes open, wishing she could stop time. Wishing she could live this day again and again. Her first happy day on earth. There was a constant smile on her face the entire night. It was then that she asked herself why she didn't have a family. A mother, a father, and perhaps one sibling. She used to stand a minute extra after school only to check out the parents who came to take their children home. Home: a concept she had not been exposed to yet in life. Hostel isn't home, that she knew well.

The happiness on the students' faces while walking home with their parents was something she coveted. When they opened their tiffin boxes during recess, they proudly told everyone what their mother had prepared. Not her. Or any other orphan. She did ask the warden a few times about her family. All she was told was that she was found by the roadside in Nellore. The person who used to work at the orphanage as a janitor was kind enough to bring her there. Trying to imagine how her mother would have been, how her father would have been, giving them faces in her imagination, the orphan teen didn't know when she fell asleep on her birthday night.

She wasn't sure what woke her up. Was it a nudge from the warden or the sound of incessant rain outside? Opening her eyes properly, the orphan teen realized it was a bit of both. The female warden was standing next to her bed in an ominous manner. The orphan teen sat up on her bed; alert and folding her hands around her bosom.

'Come down. Your birthday gift is waiting,' the warden said and went out. The orphan teen, without changing her night clothes, followed her out with both eagerness and child-like excitement. No one had given her a gift before.

She reached the warden's cabin on the ground floor to see the history and science teachers laughing at some joke. They then smiled looking at her. She stood clueless.

'Your science teacher wanted to gift you something,' the history teacher said.

'Let's go,' the science teacher said.

'The gift is outside?' she asked.

The two nodded. They had the same gleam in their eyes that she had seen when they had exorcised the ghost from her a year ago. It was just that her naive mind still hadn't understood what was evil and what was not, or how to identify one from the other.

The orphan teen went out with them. The two had an umbrella each. All along the way, they kept pushing her from one umbrella to the other as if she was a ball.

'Where are we going, sir?' the orphan teen asked. The rain was scaring her. And the continuous lightning and thunder made her shudder each time.

'We wanted to make your birthday memorable. You know what memorable is?'

The orphan teen nodded and said after a peal of thunder, 'Something that you can't forget.'

'Exactly. See, she is a sharp kid,' the history teacher told the science teacher. They laughed together. There was something condescending about their laugh. She couldn't decipher what it was, but it did make her uncomfortable.

They reached a place under a tree by a road. The rain was beating down relentlessly, punctuated by constant lightning.

The history teacher took out an iron rod from the bag he was carrying and handed it to her. The orphan teen grabbed the iron road with sincerity. She didn't want to let them down.

'Just go out there and stand in that pool of water holding this. And watch some magic happen,' the science teacher said. There was a little reluctance in the orphan teen because of the incessant rain. The thunder was scary while the lightning was such that time and again it made her shut her eyes tight in fear.

'Don't worry, we are here only. Go on now,' the history teacher said. With nervous steps and holding on to the rod, the orphan teen went out of the tree's expanse. She stepped into the puddle of water, getting drenched in the process. The cold wind along with the rain had given her goosebumps all over. Her frock was flying high. She stood there in the water puddle, not knowing that at any moment lightning could not only pass through the iron rod but also through her. Her teachers had turned her into a human lightning conductor for fun.

As the orphan teen turned to look at them, clueless as to what kind of gift they were giving her, she saw them laughing their hearts out. Her fear was their pleasure.

And when the lightning struck, thrice in a row, the orphan teen thought she wouldn't live any longer. The teachers were right. She would never forget that night, if she would still be alive . . . or maybe the magic that her science teacher was talking about was about her remaining alive, come what may. The child still wanted to give the adults the benefit of the doubt.

* * *

Chapter 17

'Shravan is now dead,' Naishee's voice was fragile as she spoke. Though the room's light was off, a little light from the neighbourhood that was peeping into the room told Ashwath that Naishee was shivering quite vigorously. Her breaths were short and rapid. He tried to hug her but she pushed him away.

'Don't touch me,' Naishee said.

Ashwath took a deep breath. He suddenly felt acutely guilty. The video was enough for him to guess that burying Shravan alive had happened because the police had been officially triggered. By him. The placard had clearly stated that. Should he tell her now or later? Or at all?

'Why would he kill him now? I was following everything he was asking me to do. I did pass in the last question. Or . . .'

Naishee looked up at Ashwath as if something had struck her, 'Was Shravan killed because I had pills against the kidnapper's wish? He hadn't said anything about it.'

There was silence. She went close to him.

'It means I'm responsible for my brother's death. Such a wretched sister I am, Ash,' Naishee broke down sitting on the bed. Ashwath couldn't take it. His guilt, mixed with Naishee's wrong interpretation of it all, was tearing his heart apart. Quite impulsively, he spoke up.

'Shravan didn't die because of you. He died . . .' A pause later, he added, 'because of me.'

There was no immediate reaction. Naishee thought she had heard him totally wrong. There was no time for anything more absurd at the moment. She broke the embrace. Ashwath wiped the sweat from his forehead even though the fan was on.

'What the fuck do you mean?' she asked.

'Look, I did it because I couldn't see you suffer any more. Seeing you like this—'

'Cut the crap, Ashwath. Tell me, what did you do?'

'I talked to one of my friends who knew someone in the cybercrime unit of the Chennai police. I got in touch with them. They took the email ID from me and followed up with Gita Vidyashram.'

Naishee had an 'I-don't-know-what-to-say' look of disgust on her face.

'I know I should have told you, but I didn't know it would lead to—' Ashwath was cut short by a fierce Naishee.

'You didn't know? Why do you think I wasn't involving the police all these days and was undergoing the shit myself? The kidnapper has Shravan buried inside a grave with his limbs tied and his mouth stuffed. He is playing some sadistic game with me. It's clear whoever is behind all this is a psycho. Maybe he doesn't have a motive. Maybe he simply loves toying with people like this. All this would have come out if I did what he asked me to without involving the police. Shravan was at his mercy, Ash. So was I. Tell me, didn't you realize all this?'

'I did. But—'

'Ashwath, just leave.'

'Naishee, please listen—'

'Right now!' Naishee almost screamed her lungs out. Ashwath remained quiet for a few seconds and then left the flat.

Naishee could feel palpable anger within her. She wanted to smash something. But all she could do was dig her face into the pillow.

Standing outside the apartment building, Ashwath called the cybercrime unit officer to cross-check if they had indeed nabbed someone from Gita Vidyashram. If there was something that would redeem him in front of Naishee, it had to be the fact that the cybercrime unit had caught the kidnapper. Nothing else, Ashwath had a feeling, would make Naishee accept him back. It was there in her eyes that he had let her down. Unknowingly, perhaps, but still it was a letdown in a big way.

'We did take a man named Swamy into custody. He is the one who is responsible for opening the emails in Gita Vidyashram. He works there. He denied opening any email ID with Naishee's name. In fact, our team did check the computer. The email wasn't opened from that machine even though the IP was the same.'

'Is that possible?'

'It is. The person must have used the school's Wi-Fi to access the emails or hacked into the system to do so. In either of the scenarios, it's not possible to pinpoint the exact person. We checked the CCTV footage of the school as well. The day you mentioned the email was sent, no one other than Swamy had used the machine. We even hacked into the email ID to learn that the email was opened using a laptop, not a phone. And proxy servers were used.'

Ashwath suddenly felt his head becoming heavy listening to the officer.

'What do we do now?' he asked, praying the officer would give him a solid way ahead.

'We are keeping an eye on Swamy to see if he is up to anything untoward, but considering whatever you told me about the kidnapping, he doesn't look like someone who can pull this off. Not alone at least.'

'Why?'

'He has polio in his left hand and leg. At best he can be an accomplice. Or he may have accomplices.'

Ashwath let out a sigh.

'I'll call if we get anything,' the officer said and ended the call. Ashwath looked up at Naishee's window. He couldn't go in now. The only thing he had been counting on had fallen flat. He called a friend in BTM Layout and decided to put up there for the time being.

The next day, Mani and Meenakshi were both happily surprised to see Naishee come home. Meenakshi in particular hugged her tight. Naishee realized her hug wasn't just an 'I-missed-you' hug, as it used to be before. It was more of a 'we-need-you-here' hug. Naishee had intentionally avoided meeting her parents all these days because she was sure their presence would make her weak. And that was one thing she couldn't afford while executing the sadistic games of the kidnapper. Now, everything was anyway lost.

Naishee didn't announce anything immediately. She prepared tea for her parents, then sat down with them in the hall. Somehow she felt they had accepted that Shravan wouldn't return. More so when she heard her father speak up with guilt.

'Tell me, Naishee, did Shravan leave on his own because I scolded him about the gay thing?' Mani sounded broken.

Naishee wondered whether Shravan's absence was making her father introspective. She kept her teacup on the table in front of her and walked to him. She held his hand and said, 'Appa, now all of that doesn't matter.' She took a deep breath. She had to say it out loud.

'Shravan is no more.'

Meenakshi dropped her teacup with a thud on the table. It broke into pieces while the tea spilt out. She dashed out of the hall. Mani sat still. Quiet. Frozen.

'How do you know?' Mani asked after some time.

'Isn't it evident? He was seen collapsing into the manhole but his body wasn't found, ever. He didn't just fall. It was a trap. Someone preyed on him. I don't know why. And the why, anyway, isn't going to bring him back. I've accepted it; you guys do it as well. The sooner the better.' Naishee said. Every word she said was breaking her heart further but she had to be strong as well. She couldn't possibly tell them what their daughter had gone through. It would ruin their mental health once and for all.

Though Meenakshi wasn't ready to accept it, it took Naishee two to three days and tons of conversation to explain that it was better to accept what is than live in a bubble of false hope. It was only when Mani told his wife that their daughter was perhaps right somewhere, that she gave in reluctantly.

Since they didn't have Shravan's dead body, they couldn't perform any funeral. Four days later, a prayer meeting was arranged by Naishee herself. Her parents had still not accepted the fact. Truth be told, Naishee too wouldn't have accepted it if she hadn't seen the video. The entire locality had come, including Shravan's friends from school and a few teachers. The next day, Naishee booked tickets for her parents and herself to Bengaluru. This house couldn't be 'home' for them any more. Not this soon. And she didn't want to leave her parents alone there. After she had told them about Shravan, they seemed to have aged further.

On the train, she felt a little discomfort in her stomach. When she went to the washroom, Naishee realized her period had finally arrived. There was relief but it couldn't eclipse the sadness that Shravan's death had brought her.

* * *

Chapter 18

Three months had gone by. Naishee had somehow moved out of the first phase of emotional trauma, that of denial. Her parents had been with her till the last month. They could see how she was going the extra mile, pushing herself to keep them occupied and feeling bereft with loneliness. This was also the time when Naishee told her father where she worked. Mani didn't say anything except, 'Do what you feel is right for yourself.' Naishee realized he was already a changed man. Loss does to humans what nothing else can do.

It was Mani in particular, who felt uncomfortable when he learnt that Naishee had said 'no' to two events because she would have to travel, leaving her parents behind. From her parents' point of view, she was sacrificing for them, which she was, but the other half of that truth was that she herself wasn't confident about living alone anywhere. From a happy family, they had suddenly been turned into a broken one. A collective scar had been imposed on them. And everyone in their own way was trying to seal the broken area but in vain.

Mani never got the time or chance to even put forward his opinion from the time he learnt that Naishee was living in Bengaluru instead of Hyderabad and that she wasn't pursuing a career in software engineering any more. And now, when he could see her passionately indulge in her photography work, Mani realized that perhaps he had been too strict with her.

'It's her life after all. All the more important that she should figure it out.'

Mani and Meenakshi appreciated everything that their daughter was doing but, one day, when Naishee went to the office, her parents did talk among themselves about whether they were becoming an obstacle for their daughter to follow her passion. Mani, in particular, seemed to have become a changed man. He had lost one child. He didn't want to lose another. That evening, when Naishee came back from work, she noticed her parents had packed their bags.

'What's this all about?'

'I think it's best for all of us that we get back to our original life,' Mani said. 'This forced change is not going to last for a long term. Better we . . . move on. You have your own life now. If we don't allow normality to prevail, then we will go on pretending that all's well.'

Naishee could understand how much her father's heart must have pained to utter the last two words. She didn't say anything; she just went to her room, had a shower and came out with a decision.

'You're right, appa. We will forever miss Shravan, anyway. But we can't remain stuck either.'

The next day, her parents took the bus to Karur, while Naishee continued immersing herself in work. A two-day gala corporate event was supposed to happen in Pune. She joined her entire team in Pune's Ritz-Carlton where they were put up. They were happy to finally have her travel with them. Ashwath was still staying with a friend. Their talks had reduced both on WhatsApp and on call. They hadn't met since the day Ashwath left the flat at Naishee's behest.

When she'd gone home last to bring her parents here, Naishee had messaged Ashwath telling him that he should come and collect his stuff in a day and leave the spare keys with the guard. Ashwath did as asked without raising any questions or even trying to appease her in any way. Their relationship remained intact like a book on a shelf. Both had no time for it— neither to clean up the dust it was gathering every day, nor to open and continue reading it from where they both had closed it.

It was in between the last heads of department meeting in the boardroom of the Ritz-Carlton that Naishee excused herself to go to the washroom. It seemed empty when she stepped in. But immediately, she heard the whimpering cries of a woman. It was odd but Naishee went ahead and entered a toilet cubicle. While she was relieving herself, she could sense the lady in the adjacent toilet had moved out. As Naishee pushed the flush button, tugged her panties up and moved out, she paused seeing DK. The latter too glanced at her via the mirror in front of her. It was clear DK had not expected to see her there.

'Everything all right, DK?' Naishee asked, getting closer. There was a momentary eye lock between them. DK pulled out a few tissues, wiped her hands, threw them in the dustbin and then walked out, all in one breath.

Naishee went back to work with the temptation of asking DK if she needed her. But she didn't. After all, she was only one of DK's employees. She also understood something personal must have happened. The powerful boss lady that DK was, Naishee had never associated her with the crying-in-the-washroom kind. Naishee carried on with the event work and went back to her room at around 3 a.m. She was exhausted but sleep wasn't coming to her. This was the most dangerous hour for anyone who was running from something within oneself. It's an hour when one feels the loneliest and most defeatist.

Naishee threw herself on the bed, took out her phone and indulged in what had come to be the global timepass: scrolling social media. She noticed Ashwath had uploaded a short reel. It was from a stand-up stint of his. She couldn't help but smile on hearing the content. The guy was talented. From the time she'd asked him, en route to Karur to get her parents to Bengaluru, to shift his stuff out from her place, Ashwath had not messaged or called to appease her. He had not even put up those social media likes that one did to subtly announce one's presence lest she forget him. That way, he was a mature guy. But did it also mean he had moved on from here that easily? Did it rub his male ego so much that he wouldn't be back ever? Was something even possible between them in the future? Would she be able to accept him back in her life knowing he was responsible, in an indirect but sure way, for the death of her brother? Too many thoughts at once. Naishee compulsively opened Ashwath's WhatsApp chat window and stared at it, trying to think of what to message him. Then she closed the chat window, kept the phone down and lay back, closing her eyes. A minute later, she heard a notification buzz. It was DK's message.

Slept?

Naishee responded: *Nope. All good?*

Can you please come to my room?

Naishee thought before replying. A few minutes later, she was in DK's room. It stank of whisky and cigarettes.

'Come, Naishee. Sit here.' DK's voice was solemn. Naishee did as asked. She took the chair by the study table while noticing DK was perched on one corner of the couch with her legs stretched out.

'Nothing of what I tell you goes out of this room, Naishee.'

'Hmm.' She understood something deeply personal was coming. As Naishee eyes got used to the darkness in the room, she realized DK looked poised but something was wrong. As if she was forcing the poise. She hadn't felt such contradictory vibes from DK before.

'And, just listen. Don't ask. Don't speak. Don't interrupt.'

'Okay.'

'I had a hot flash, that's why I was crying in the washroom. I mean, that wasn't the reason really. I have been having these hot flashes for some time now. I did consult a doctor. I'm heading towards my menopause. I know you won't understand it now. You're at your prime. Probably with a steady boyfriend.'

There was silence. Naishee did feel a little awkward when DK wondered whether she had a steady boyfriend. Naishee was never the kind to discuss her personal life with her professional boss or colleagues. Nor was DK till then.

DK continued, 'I don't know where to begin tonight. It's not just the menopause thing. Would you believe I never had a boyfriend in my life? I mean, not a steady one. I was always ambitious and thus I got men who either wanted to rip off my ambitious nature or manipulate me to slow down because their nincompoop male ego couldn't take it that a woman was better than them. And why should I blame them alone? I've tried so much but my life never remained normal. Since childhood I was...' DK went on and on and on about how difficult her life had been. Especially her dalliances with men and now she had no one. Naishee heard her patiently but there was something deeply disturbing in the way DK was talking and everything she was talking about. It wasn't just a woman talking about her past. It was an individual, a woman reflecting on how bitchy society can be towards women at different phases of life. For every decade of a girl's life is different. With a different set of roles and a defined set of expectations.

DK's rant ended after a good fifty minutes.

Naishee came back to her room and slumped on the bed. The woman she had met in DK's room was not the aspirational, successful lady she used to meet in the office, or for that matter, anyone in the company. This was someone who had become hollow from within. Her soul seemed captive within the frame of sadness and loneliness. Not her fault entirely but Naishee didn't want to be like her at her age. She couldn't be lonely like her. Work or the ability to work fades one day and then you need someone . . . a companion, she thought. Else, like DK, she too would be calling those working with or under her in the middle of the night and ranting about her inner turmoil. No, she couldn't allow that to happen. It was too sordid a picture of a woman she had seen in the room. Naishee wasn't ready to accept it.

An impulse made her open her phone and message Ashwath a 'Hi'. She kept waiting the entire night but no response came. He hadn't checked the message. In the morning, she took a shower, not able to keep DK's voice out of her mind, then got dressed and left for Bengaluru with her teammates.

Naishee entered her flat continuously yawning. It was a day off for everyone in the office. She didn't even care to change. Ashwath's response in the form of a 'Hi' had come when she was on the flight. She had read it while disembarking but didn't reply.

She kept her baggage in the hall room and sauntered to the bedroom. She got into bed immediately. As she tried to place her head on the soft pillow, she hit something hard under it. A quick check told her it wasn't under the pillow but inside its cover.

Naishee sat up with her heart racing as she took out a parcel. She tore it open and brought out a mobile phone, the same brand as she used to receive before. She switched the phone on. The photo gallery this time had only one video. And the video had three placards.

The first read: *It's Shravan's birthday the day after tomorrow.*

The second read: *Do you want to wish him? He said his akka never misses his birthday.*

The third read: *If yes, wave a white cloth from your terrace in the next twenty-four hours.*

* * *

Chapter 19

Naishee rushed out of bed, opened her wardrobe and pulled out a white shirt. She grabbed it tight and ran to the apartment's terrace. She started waving the white shirt as asked. She had no idea if she was being watched. In reality, she was. Not by the orphan lady though. She'd hired some men who were carrying out some work on her behalf for money. One of those was the man who used to sit by the tea shop right outside Naishee's apartment and keep an eye on her, relaying every bit to the orphan lady. He was the one who had placed the parcel with the guard the first time, in the milk pouch the second time, and it was him who had also managed to barge into her flat the third time when she was in Goa. Only to Goa had the orphan lady travelled herself. It was too important an activity to be left to some paid proxy. Moreover, she couldn't let a man torture a girl ever.

Naishee's mind was overjoyed with only one fact: Shravan was alive. That's all she needed to know to reconnect to happiness in life. She messaged Ashwath and asked him to come home immediately. He didn't ask nor did she clarify. He was taken aback for sure. Her excitement told him that something good must have happened.

It was one of the most difficult waits for her. Every minute she wanted to pick up her phone and call Ashwath or her parents and tell them . . . scream it aloud actually, that Shravan was alive, unlike what they were thinking. It also meant the sadistic game wasn't over but she would take care of it later. For now, she just wanted to savour the moment and be happy.

When the doorbell rang, Naishee jumped up from the couch to open the door. Ashwath had no clue what was awaiting him. In his mind, he was rehearsing how he would apologize once again, if need be, and try to sort things out, for his gut told him this was the last chance Naishee would give him to get back in her life. And from here, he would have to be really careful. The only reason he didn't approach Naishee until then was that he knew she wasn't the kind who appreciated clinginess. If she said she didn't want him around, she didn't want him around. Now when she called him on her own, she definitely would have meant she wanted him around. As he kept going through a rough monologue of sorts that he had prepared on the way, the moment the door opened, it seemed to him as if a bottled-up energy was unleashed on him. He was pulled in and the door was closed before he knew it.

'Naishee?' Ashwath just muttered after which he felt her lips on his. She took his hands and placed them on her breasts. He started squeezing them. As they smooched urgently with him against the main door, one of the latches started hurting him.

'Let's go inside, please,' he said.

'Cool. Don't waste time eating me. I'm too wet. Fuck me silly,' Naishee said, held his hand and pulled him into the bedroom.

Damn, I missed you, Naishee thought, feeling his hardness inside her.

'Fuck, I've never felt you that wet,' Ashwath seemed genuinely surprised. Naishee managed a giggle before saying, 'No talk now. Fuck me, tiger.' She wrapped her legs around his waist and hands around his back, clawing it, feeling his thrusts increase in speed and force.

Half an hour later, they were both spent. Naishee was smiling from ear to ear. After a long time, she had felt the pleasure hormones in her body. She turned and placed her head on his chest.

'You do realize, right, that I have no idea what the fuck is happening? I just feel like some fuck toy whom you ordered and fucked,' Ashwath said.

Naishee laughed and pulled his nipple.

'Ouch!' he shrieked. 'Care to explain now what happened? Don't tell me the days of distancing were mere foreplay,' Ashwath said, pulling her closer into his chest.

Naishee looked up at him and said in a semi-choked voice, 'Shravan is alive.'

Ashwath moved in a way that disturbed their romantic posture to look at her.

'It's true. I received another parcel from the kidnapper, who told me that if I wanted to wish Shravan on his birthday, I had to wave a white cloth from my terrace.'

'Does that mean you're being watched?' Ashwath asked.

'Maybe I am. And frankly, that doesn't surprise me. The way the parcels were sent to me told me the kidnapper wanted to make it clear that he is aware of my daily movements. In fact, I received today's parcel inside my pillow.'

'Inside the pillow?' Ashwath couldn't hide his shock.

Naishee nodded. 'The one we have our heads on right now.'

Ashwath found the entire thing spooky.

'You think we should get CCTV cams inside your flat?'

'It's not my flat. I'm here on rent. And if my landlord gets even an inkling of what's happening, I shall be thrown out.'

'Hmm.' Ashwath knew she had a point. 'When is Shravan's birthday?' Ashwath asked.

'Two days from now.'

Ashwath was quiet. Naishee came closer till he could feel her breath on his face.

'I'm sorry, Ash. Not because of what I did or how I behaved. I think any sister would react that way and I hope you understand that.'

'I do.'

'I'm sorry for not considering the fact that you were trying to help me. I think I missed that point altogether in whatever happened.'

'I never blamed you once, trust me. I was just waiting.'

She kissed his chest. His phone rang. Both smiled. It had become an inside joke between them that whenever they made out, someone or the other would call one of them. This time it was Ashwath's phone. He picked up his phone from the other corner of the bed. It was his father. Naishee noticed his face change. He didn't take the call. He put his phone on airplane mode and came back to her with a smile.

'All good?' she asked. Ashwath thought for a moment and realized this was the opportune moment for him to convey what Naishee should have known by now.

'No,' he let out a sigh and said, 'My parents don't want me to marry you. After whatever has happened with Shravan and with you being absent for a month.'

Naishee didn't react immediately. She got up, put on her panties, her tee and went out. Ashwath understood she needed time. Sometime later, Naishee came in with two mugs of coffee. Ashwath sat up on the bed and took one of the mugs.

'Have they told my parents about it?'

'I don't know. I didn't ask. All I told my father is I'm not going to marry anyone else but you.'

'But they have a point, Ash,' Naishee said.

'So do I.'

Naishee came close, linked her eyes with his and held his hand. 'Are you sure, Ash?'

He clasped her hand tightly and said, 'More than sure.'

They made out immediately after they finished their coffee. This was more emotional than the session they had when Ashwath had just arrived. Then they lay down naked beside each other again. Neither knew when they fell asleep in that position.

In the morning, when Naishee stepped out to get some vegetables from the vendor on wheels by the gate, a street dog came up to her barking. Thanks to Shravan, she too had become an animal-friendly person. She noticed the dog had a shoelace tied around its neck, which was further tied to a small parcel. She frowned. As the dog kept barking, she knelt down, patted its head and slowly took the parcel. It resembled the kind she had been receiving. The man by the tea shop was watching her. By the time she found a phone inside—of the same model—Naishee had guessed it must have instructions on how she could wish Shravan on his birthday. As on the previous occasions, there was only one video. As she played the video, she stood confused.

In the video, she had instructions about what she was supposed to do next. Naishee thought hard for a moment. She knew she would do anything to talk to Shravan. But at that moment, she didn't realize it would bring death eye to eye with her.

* * *

Chapter 20

Naishee came upstairs with the veggies, went to the kitchen and started cooking. She was quickly making plans about how she would squeeze time out to execute what the kidnapper had demanded of her if she wished to save her brother.

A little later, Ashwath lazily came into the kitchen and snuggled up behind her. 'What's your plan for the day, Ash?' Naishee asked.

'To be with you the whole day.'

Naishee turned and they shared a quick kiss.

'But I have to go to office, babe. Chop this one, please,' Naishee said and put him to work. Together they ended up preparing both lunch and dinner for the day in one go. Naishee stuffed her tiffin boxes and got ready for a shower.

'I think I'll go to some café, sit for a bit and write a sketch.'

'What about that competition you had told me about?' Naishee put her towel on her shoulder, went to her wardrobe and got busy selecting the dress she would wear to the office.

'They have opened up. I've submitted my video. Fingers crossed now.' Ashwath said.

Naishee placed the dress she'd selected on her bed, then came up to him, gave him a peck and said, 'You'll get through the competition for sure.' It was a competition that was beginning its new season on a premium OTT platform. Any stand-up comic who was featured in it and did well was bound to get a wider viewership base and win a content contract with them.

'Tell me something, did your parents say anything after I had told them, when you were gone for a month, that I was doing stand-up?'

Naishee stopped by the bathroom door, turned and said with a smile, 'They didn't. They won't. They've understood the hard way that parents shouldn't interfere with their kids' career choice. How about yours?'

Ashwath smiled in a naughty manner and said, 'They still don't know what I'm up to. Don't think they need to right now either.'

Naishee smiled back and entered the bathroom. The moment she closed the door behind her, Naishee relaxed. She was finding it tough to put up a casual face in front of Ashwath with every minute. By the time she had come upstairs after buying the veggies, she had made a decision. She would not tell Ashwath about the next activity that the kidnapper wanted her to do. She had understood the last time that the kidnapper had not taken the obvious step of killing Shravan. That was a warning. But there may not be a next time. This and every activity after this, if at all, would be the last chance to keep her brother alive till the goddamn exam got over.

The video on the phone that the street dog had brought to her had two things in it. One was what she had to do next to hear her brother. Naishee's heart had skipped learning about the possibility that she could talk to Shravan. And two, she had to answer another question. It was for twenty marks and she had to score a minimum of twelve. The question was a generic one again: *Do you think humans are just evil? Or is there any goodness in them?*

Naishee opened the tap. As the bucket started filling up with water, Naishee stood with her back to the wall. She took out the paper along with a pen that she had brought into the bathroom secretly. She began writing her answer:

I don't think humans are basically evil. We all have goodness. Sometimes it's the situation that makes one evil, I guess. But no one is born with an evil mind. A lot of people I know have had a bad childhood, which turned their adult form into something evil, perhaps because of something they saw while growing up. Not all of us are lucky to have good parents. Parenting anyway is so underrated in India. Most of the evil or negative traits in adults are a result of regressive parenting. So, to answer the question, I certainly don't think people are born evil. However, they can turn evil at any given point in time depending on certain factors.

Naishee re-read it twice. It was a safe answer. Neither too liberal, nor too opinionated. Then she clicked a picture of the sheet with her answer, attached it to an email and sent it to . . . herself. That was the catch that surprised her. This time, the kidnapper had asked her to mail it to her own email ID. It could mean two things: one, he knew her password and would log in later, or two, he would have hacked into her email. Was it possible for him to know her password? Not at all.

Naishee flushed the sheet down the toilet. Then stepped into the shower naked. When she came out, she saw Ashwath by the bedroom window, pacing up and down. He looked irked and edgy.

'What happened?' She tossed the towel on the bed and put on the dress she had chosen before going to the bathroom.

'My father had a heart attack,' Ashwath said.

'Oh. You want me to—'

'He is lying.'

'What? How do you know?'

'I asked for a video call and he wasn't ready to talk.'

'Maybe he isn't comfortable.'

'I know my father, Naishee. All he wants right now in life is to get me married off to some other girl. That's all. He has done this all his life. Steered every decision of mine to the outcome he wanted. The only decisions I've taken till now of my own will are to become a stand-up comic and to love you. Anyway, appa wants me to be there so he can make me meet some prospective girls.'

Naishee thought for some time while getting ready for the office. When she was done, she said, 'Still, he is your father. I think you should go home, Ash.'

'That's the fuck-up. I'll have to go.'

Naishee went to the office while Ashwath packed his bag and went to the Bengaluru railway station. He would take the first train to Chennai and come back on the first one the day after. Or so he told himself.

In the office, Naishee went to the tech team and met the lady who headed it, Sambhavi.

'Is there any way I can locate the person who is accessing my mails?' Naishee asked. Sambhavi opened her Gmail on her laptop and showed Naishee the lower bottom part where it displays from where all the email has been accessed. At that moment, it was only showing Naishee's office location and that it was open on her mobile phone too. The email she had sent to herself was still unread. If and when it was read, that would be a signal that the kidnapper has accessed her email. Naishee kept an eye on it while attending work meetings. She had not met DK after that one night when the latter let off her emotional steam in front of her. She did see her in the office but couldn't get any personal time with her. Naishee wasn't interested in probing the matter any more. Of course, it was deeply personal and all DK needed was a pair of ears. Naishee had given her that. End of story. Perhaps DK too wasn't comfortable any longer with Naishee because of the side she had shown her that night. Naishee let it pass.

While leaving the office, accompanying one of her colleagues for a chit-chat and a smoke, Naishee saw the email had been read. And a response had come too.

Your score: 16. Expected a better answer from you. All humans are born evil. Only some get good parenting and good situations and hence they behave better. It was contrary to what Naishee had written. That one line—all humans are born evil—told Naishee the kidnapper was a misanthropist. She quickly called Sambhavi to know her coordinates. Thankfully she hadn't left the office building yet. Naishee asked her to wait. She ran upstairs and showed her the email along with the IP it was showing. To a disheartened Naishee, Sambhavi said that the IP had been masked. It wasn't possible to know if the email had been hacked or simply accessed. She advised her to change her passwords.

'Sure,' Naishee said but knew changing passwords wouldn't change anything. With disappointment as she collected her belongings and was leaving the office floor, Naishee passed by DK's cabin to reach the exit. One glance and she saw her boss waving at her through the glass wall. Naishee waved back with a tight smile. While going down in the elevator, she checked the email again. There were location coordinates along with a date and time for her to be present. Naishee took a screenshot of it for handy access. The date was Shravan's birthday.

The time was 11 p.m. The last hour of Shravan's birthday that year. Naishee had still not told Ashwath where she was heading. But unlike the last time when she was trapped in a container, this time Naishee did leave the coordinates given to her on a paste-it in her room. If she didn't return, Ashwath would most definitely reach her flat and at least know where she had gone. He was still in Chennai trying his best to negate his parents and be back soon.

Shravan's birthday also happened to be the first day of the monsoon. It had been raining hard since morning. It made it all the more difficult for Naishee to reach the location. It was a building in one of the areas of old Bengaluru. Unlike what she thought it would be, the place was bustling with people. Even the apartment building in the location coordinates was crowded with people. It looked like a government quarters of sorts.

Clueless as to what she should do there or who she should talk to, Naishee received an email from herself right when she was standing by the society gate.

Tell the guard some random flat number and go to the terrace of Building A.

Naishee did as she was told. She also kept looking around to see if she could recognize anyone, or if anyone seemed a tiny bit suspicious. Of course, the timing of the email pop-up wasn't a coincidence. Someone was registering every step of hers. She found no one or nothing eyebrow-raising.

Naishee's mind was flooded with all sorts of questions. Was Shravan being kept captive here? There was an old security guard who seemed least interested in who was going where. Naishee went inside the society and headed to building A. The moment she entered, the security guard, who was working for the orphan lady for some bucks, called a number and relayed the information. Just as he had done when he noticed Naishee standing in front of the main gate.

The entry of the building was small. It was an old building that desperately needed repair. The walls looked dirty and had several cracks. When she'd started from her place it was drizzling, but by the time she arrived here, the rain had turned incessant along with the associated lightning and thunder. Naishee was finding it difficult to hold on to her umbrella till she stepped inside building A.

Naishee reached the terrace on the fifth floor. The door was half broken and open. A fierce wind was hitting it against the wall, making a constant noise. Naishee came up to the terrace door and then, holding it open, she peeped out. There was no one there. A notification came on her phone. It was another email from herself that read: *Outside, there's a pair of shoes, wear them, get rid of the umbrella and stand in an attention pose under the rain. If you are alive for the next whole hour, you talk to your brother. Else, wish you a happy death.*

Naishee swallowed a lump. *How can wearing a pair of shoes kill someone?* she thought. With a frown, Naishee stepped on to the terrace. She looked around and noticed a pair of shoes in one corner. They were getting drenched. Holding the umbrella tight, she took off her shoes and then wore the ones kept there. As Naishee's feet touched the soles, she understood that the shoes had an iron base. She kept the umbrella aside. Getting drenched in the rain, she looked around. She couldn't locate any lightning conductor on the old building. Then it struck her. Nothing had to be explained to her any more. Everything was clear. She was going to die in the next one hour.

Chapter 21

Standing under the heavy rain, Naishee could hear her heart thumping inside her. Even though she was there so she could hear her brother speak, at that moment Naishee was sure it was a mistake to listen to the kidnapper. She understood what she had been turned into—a human lightning conductor. Why had she been asked to come to the terrace of this building exactly? An aged building like this must have done away with its lightning conductor. Or maybe it never had one. Or maybe the kidnapper had removed it. Her instinct was to simply run to the terrace's door which she could see in the distance from where she was standing. But that would also mean no talk with Shravan. It could also mean Shravan being buried alive finally for she would have not executed the activity as asked. Then she wondered whether she would really get to talk to him or if it was another of those sadistic games of the kidnapper. That's when the first bolt of lightning struck. Naishee had gooseflesh immediately. Every flash of lightning had an equal probability of burning her through. And every time she was saved, she couldn't relax for she didn't how many more she had to survive for the next one hour.

After some time, Naishee started feeling cold because of the rain and the breeze which had turned into a strong wind. In all, there were six strong lightning bolts in the span of that one hour. None of them hurt her. It was pure luck. That's what the kidnapper had meant when he wrote, '*If you are alive for the next whole hour, you talk to your brother.*' The *if* factor. When she survived the fourth, she had tears in her eyes. She had to beat destiny to talk to Shravan. And she had done it. The first part was over as Naishee removed the iron shoes and ran barefoot to the terrace door the moment one hour was up. She put her shoes back on and rushed down the stairs of the terrace when her phone rang. She noticed it was a video call, an Internet call from one of the messenger apps she used. Naishee stopped. Took a breather and then took the call. It was Shravan on the screen.

She could have cried then and there.

'Akka, talk to me please. We have a minute,' he said.

'Murali! I love you, brother. How are you?' She didn't want to but she was crying.

'I'm alive. Just alive. How are you, akka? I miss you and everyone.'

Before any important questions could be asked or answered, the one minute had gone by. Naishee managed to squeeze in a 'happy birthday' to him and told him she would free him. He asked her to promise him that and she did. The video call ended exactly in one minute. Naishee tried to call back but it didn't go through. Not that she was expecting it to. At least the kidnapper had kept his word. Shravan was still in captivity and yet Naishee felt slightly relieved realizing something. The kidnapper had kept his word, she thought, which meant she could safely assume that if she passed the exam, Shravan would be free. She could do with such a possibility at the moment.

While going back home, Naishee was fighting the urge to let her parents know that Shravan was alive. But she didn't tell them. There would be a hundred questions from them, which she was not in a position to answer. They had somehow accepted that Shravan was probably dead when she had suggested it, but now if she told them he was alive, they wouldn't rest in peace without knowing about the source of the information. Naishee had only had a talk with Shravan right now. A positive step after all these months but the thing wasn't over. He was still being held captive god knows where. The talk, however, gave her renewed hope that her brother would not only live but, in all probability, would also be with their family one day soon. Naishee remembered the exam. Full marks were 100. Till now she had answered three questions worth twenty, twenty-five and twenty marks each. It meant another thirty-five marks were left. Whether the thirty-five marks would have three questions, five or ten, Naishee didn't know. All she knew was that until she didn't answer all the questions, scored the necessary marks and then held Shravan herself, she couldn't afford to involve anyone else. She had still not forgotten the feeling when she saw earth being thrown on Shravan's face in the video leading her to believe he was dead. All she had to do now was wait for the next parcel from the kidnapper.

The rain had subsided but the traffic had become worse. Sitting in her Uber, she kept playing Shravan's video call in her mind. He didn't look as badly affected as she thought he would be. There weren't any marks of violence on his face, which was good. His hair had grown, for sure. Maybe the kidnapper was giving him food on time. His staying alive was as important to her as it was to the kidnapper, she thought. At least till the exam was on. But she still couldn't surmise any plausible reason why anyone would want to harm someone as innocent as Shravan and make his sister undergo an exam. Even if he was the bait, then who was the target? She?

That night, Naishee had the most amazing sleep after ages. She woke up fresh and saw the message that Ashwath was travelling back to Bengaluru finally. He reached in another three hours. He looked exhausted when he came in.

'How's your father?' Naishee asked, following him to the bedroom.

'Fit as a fiddle,' he said, lying on the bed without changing.

'You met the girls he wants you to marry?'

'Yes. Three of them. And I told all of them that if I married them, they would be my second wife.'

Naishee burst out laughing.

'You can't be serious!'

'I am.'

'Come on, it's not their fault.'

'That's why I warned them beforehand. Chuck all that. I have big news. Though I got the news yesterday, I wanted to give it to you in person.'

'Will you cut the formal crap and tell me what it is?' Naishee asked. Yesterday it was Shravan's video call and now some good news from Ashwath. Life suddenly seemed better. If only slightly.

'I've made it to the stand-up comic competition,' Ashwath announced. Naishee lurched on to him, kissing him all over.

'So proud of you, Ash,' she said. 'What's next now?'

'Fifteen of us will be called to Mumbai where they will make arrangements for our lodging, etc. We will compete in front of a live audience and judges. The episodes will be shot there and later telecast on the OTT platform. The last one standing wins the competition.'

'That will be you,' she said and pecked him.

'The catch is that I'll have to be there for two months on the trot.'

'Oh, starting?'

'Soon. They'll let me know the dates. I'll miss you.'

Naishee understood what he was hinting at. She knew her company had an office in Pune, not Mumbai. If somehow she could work from there, then her meeting Ashwath wouldn't suffer.

Later that day in the office, Naishee made it a point to see DK. The latter was in her cabin, smoking away when Naishee knocked. Seeing her, DK had a smile on her face. She gestured for her to come in. Naishee entered.

'What's cooking, good-looking?' DK asked. Her vibe told Naishee that this, once again, was the successful woman who used to inspire one and all.

'All good. How have you been?'

Naishee took a seat opposite DK.

'Been steady. Acceptance is therapeutic, no?' There was an unprecedented aura about DK that Naishee wasn't able to decipher.

'I guess so,' she said.

'What would you know? You're too young to even seek any kind of healing. At your age, I was all about wounds.'

'Does being wounded depend on age?'

'It ideally doesn't. But some unlucky ones get subjected to it at a young age. At a very young age.' DK stressed the last part.

'Can I be honest?' Naishee asked.

'A lady usually shouldn't be, but in front of another lady, you just may.' DK was amused.

'We all get wounded. I don't think that is the point. The point is what we do with the wound. Do we allow it to make a mess of us? Or do we turn it into an emotional diamond, making us valuable for everyone, most importantly, our own selves?'

DK's amused expression vanished. A thoughtful one came in its place. She went silent.

'I wanted to know, DK, if I could work from the Pune office for a couple of months, please?'

DK shot a blank look at her and said, 'Sure.'

Naishee found the ease with which DK let her have her way a tad surprising. It was as if she was waiting for it. Or was she reading too much into it?

* * *

Chapter 22

Nineteen Years Ago

By now the orphan teen understood well that the history and the science teachers weren't good souls. And certainly weren't people who wanted to do her any good. She'd also found out what the 'ghost' actually meant. It was something that didn't reside in her but had made a deep home in them. Its name was Lust. No other girl in the orphanage was ever exorcised except her. With these discoveries in the last two to three years, the orphan teen had also realized one ugly truth about the world: it had ears but it heard only people who were powerful. She did try to tell the hostel warden about what the two teachers had done with her only to be rebuked in return, saying it was her mind that was polluted. No teacher could ever do something so abhorrent. The news that she'd complained against the two teachers reached them. They then locked her up in an unknown location, naked. Her exams were approaching. And they said they wouldn't let her appear for any of the exams. It was only when she cried, begged and promised them that she would never complain again, that the two teachers allowed her to move back into the hostel, in time to prepare and sit for the exams. Then they failed her in her mid-terms. When she pleaded she wouldn't repeat her complaint, they gave her bare passing marks in the final exams of standard nine. She didn't even dare to ask them why, even though she knew she had answered most of the questions correctly.

With the advent of adolescence, not only did her hormones announce themselves, but wisdom too. But as it happens with wisdom, it often is earned at the cost of one's innocence. Passing standard ten, she was relieved that she didn't have to study either history or science. Though she had selected PCM (physics, chemistry and maths) in standard eleven, none of them would be taught by the science teacher. They only taught subjects till high school. It meant she wouldn't have to go near them or even be in their sight since classes for standard eleven and twelve happened during the day, while before that it was all-morning classes.

She'd scored just enough marks to secure a seat in the science stream in standard eleven. Even before the board exams, she remembered the two teachers had taken her to the staff quarters. Then she was made to drink something which tasted shitty to her. After that, she remembered nothing except feeling some pain in her privates. Finally, things would end. The orphan teen had a rough plan of sorts in her mind. She would study for another two years, pass her standard twelve and then leave the hostel as well as Vellore. She would go to some big city like Chennai and study further while working. Away from the shit that she had been exposed to by the two teachers for years now.

One day, there was some renovation work in the hostel. Extra beds were being brought in. It surprised everyone in the hostel for the space was already less for the ones who were staying. The next day, forty more orphans came in, of different ages ranging from seven to fourteen. The orphan teen's eyes lay on a particular girl who looked visibly vulnerable. She went to her to ask what her name was.

'Arpita,' the girl said in a soft voice.

'Your age?'

'Twelve.'

The orphan teen could see her own self in her. The same softness, same innocence, and the same fear on her face. She started helping her in the hostel with whatever she needed. In the evening when everyone used to do their homework in the hostel, the orphan teen used to help her with it. She became her mother hen of sorts. It was when Arpita told her that the history teacher was fond of her, that the orphan teen became alert. Was she their fresh target now that she wasn't on their teaching radar? She felt a thud in her heart. She couldn't sleep that night. As she tossed in her bed, she could see Arpita sleeping peacefully. The orphan teen wondered if that peace would be ruined soon. How many girls have those teachers made their victims? Won't it ever stop?

On the weekend, the orphan teen noticed Arpita was all dressed up as if she was going to someone's birthday party.

'Where did you get this dress from?' she asked.

'Science sir gave it to me,' Arpita replied. The orphan teen could hear her heart thump. She noticed Arpita looking at her with some anticipation in her eyes. She shrugged.

'There's a secret. Though science and history sirs have asked me not to tell this to anyone but you always help me. I think you are a good person, like a good akka.'

For the first time, the orphan teen felt a bond had been formed. Someone had called her 'akka'. She not only felt happy but responsible as well. She kissed Arpita's forehead.

'Are they going to exorcise a ghost in you?' the orphan teen asked. Arpita seemed shocked.

'How do you know? It's a secret. Don't tell the others, else I will be kicked out,' Arpita said in a cautious manner. The orphan teen knew that the two teachers must have told her that too. She didn't say anything but kept an eye on Arpita. Around 9 p.m., Arpita was ushered by the warden out of the hostel. Half an hour later, the orphan teen managed to sneak out of the hostel herself. By now she knew all the inner workings of the hostel so she could avoid being seen by anyone. That was how a few other senior girls used to elope to meet their boyfriends.

She walked up to the staff quarters without being seen by anyone. But she didn't use the entrance of the school, which was always guarded. She went around the school premises and climbed a tree whose branches dropped inside the school. It took some time and a few nasty scratches on her body to land inside the school grounds. She scampered to the staff quarters. She knew where the science teacher stayed. Even the history teacher. They were on the ground floor.

As the orphan teen went to the back of the staff quarters, she traced the location of their rooms from behind. She looked through the closed window to see all three of them. The 'exorcism' was on, just as they had done with her. Enraged, the orphan teen ran up to the staff quarters entrance and started screaming her lungs out. The guard, the staff, everyone was alert. They came out along with the history teacher. The orphan teen complained that a new orphan had been brought to the staff quarters. Everyone went to the science teacher's room to check but found nothing. The orphan teen was scolded for breaking protocol and entering the school premises at odd hours without telling anyone.

The two teachers, however, weren't the kind to sit quietly with only one scolding. They could have actually been caught if the science teacher had not asked the kid to run out from his room's window. Thankfully the kid was smart and ran back to the hostel herself, else they could have been suspended and perhaps jailed too. They knew the orphan teen had to be punished. And she was. And this time the punishment took away her education along with her plans of doing anything worthwhile for the next two years.

* * *

Chapter 23

The parcel reached her this time in a pretty straightforward manner, in her office. When Naishee entered, the receptionist stood up excusing herself.

'This came for you, ma'am,' she said.

Naishee took the parcel, went to her seat and opened it. She didn't even care to ask the receptionist whether she had seen someone. She understood the kidnapper well enough now to know he wouldn't have those kinds of glitches where she could reach him using the courier service trail. She found a mobile phone inside. She was so used to the drill by now that she didn't waste time checking it out. She switched it on, went to the photo gallery and tapped on the video. This time the placard had the question: *Why is a woman's modesty so frivolous?* The marks indicated beside it were ten. And then came the activity that she had to perform. It shook her to her core.

She was supposed to tattoo something on her forearm. The font size was also given. And that something was a four-letter word: SLUT (in Tamil). Naishee understood that after the physical and mental horror, what she had to endure was humiliation, social and personal. Both she as well as the kidnapper knew she couldn't possibly stop participating in the activity now. Not after tasting blood. And after knowing Shravan was still alive. First things first, Naishee told herself and then wrote her answer in a mail:

I think the answer to this roots back to the fact that societal design and its rules were made by men. And it is because the male took on the role of the provider and protector to begin with. That was the single most important decision in the history of mankind. Or so I feel. The moment the male took on those roles, things never looked great for the female. We are still fighting not for what's ours, we are actually fighting for what doesn't belong to the male alone— this fucking world. We wrongly think that nature wants equality. I think nature believes in complementing. Men and women aren't equal. They are supposed to complement each other without any fixed gender roles. Sure, there should be equality of opportunities so both genders can reach their true potential and thereby complement each other to the maximum for a peaceful balance in society. But men understood that the moment women would be allowed to go beyond the gender roles they had assigned to them, men's arrogance would be squashed. And hence, it's they who made a woman's modesty frivolous. It actually isn't.

Naishee re-read it and mailed it to herself. She thought for some time and then Googled tattoo parlours near her office. She was yet to get inked. It was always a fascination but never in her wildest dreams did she think she would have to tattoo what was asked of her. She zeroed in on one tattoo parlour, called it and booked an appointment for the evening. The location of the tattoo was also predetermined in the video.

Initially, after getting SLUT tattooed on her forearm, she tried covering it up but with no success. Anyone who saw her would see the tattoo first. That was the intention of the kidnapper. To make her embarrassed. Of the tattoo. Of herself. Squash her confidence. What was the takeaway from all this? As Naishee took the metro, she could see men giving her unsavoury looks. She changed the compartment. Then the women were giving her the same looks. Naishee tried her best not to look at anyone.

While looking for an autorickshaw, she could see random men eyeing her. Even the autowallahs checked her tattoo first and then looked at her face. She could have covered it but she knew that wouldn't suffice for the kidnapper, not in public at least. And she didn't want to take a chance. Of course, she was being watched. No one could convince her otherwise. How? By whom? That she didn't know.

She reached her apartment and was surprised to see Ashwath's father, Dushyant, there. He was standing by the main gate.

'I want to talk to you,' he said and noticed the tattoo. He didn't react as Naishee withdrew her hand, covering it with her other hand.

'Sure, uncle. Let's go upstairs.' *Right things happening at the wrong time*, she thought. Naishee guessed what Ashwath's father had come here for, but he had chosen the wrong day.

As the two entered the flat, Dushyant stopped a little beyond the entrance and said, 'I'll be straight with you, Naishee. I don't know if Ashwath has already told you or not but we don't want any alliance with you. Nothing personal, it's just that—'

'I get it, uncle. I respect it as well. But I can't do much here. If Ashwath asks me to back off, I sure will. If he doesn't, no one else gets to do it,' Naishee said the last part in a way to show her determination to Dushyant.

'There, I told him that a girl who can raise her voice against an elder would never make his home peaceful.'

'I don't know, uncle, if I should say this or not, but I'm so thankful that your son Ashwath doesn't think like that.'

'Maybe it's your spell that has turned him into an idiot who can't see that a girl who has SLUT tattooed on her forearm is worth shit. What is it? Another cool way of this generation?' Dushyant said and walked off.

Naishee didn't know whether she should cry or simply laugh about the matter. She waited till Ashwath came in later at night.

'Your father was here,' she said, turning to look at him while sitting on the sofa.

'Is what he was telling me right?' he asked. Naishee had never heard such a condescending tone from him. Naishee understood Dushyant must have called him after leaving her place.

'What?'

'That you've gotten a tattoo?'

Naishee showed him the tattoo. And noticed Ashwath's visage change to a judgemental one for her.

'Won't you ask me why I got it?'

'Maybe later. Today I was trying my best to make it happen, to convince my parents that you're a good girl. And now this? You do realize this tattoo is a point of no return, right?'

Ashwath turned and left the flat in suppressed anger. Naishee had caught her breath while listening to him. As she slowly exhaled, she murmured, 'I really didn't expect you to say the last thing that you did.'

* * *

Chapter 24

Ashwath packed his bag and left for Mumbai that night itself. He had got his call from the OTT platform. He would be there for the next two months. The silence that prevailed between them, from the time Ashwath went to the bedroom until he moved out for Mumbai, scared Naishee. It's silences like these that, if stretched, have the potential to sink any relationship.

The next day at the office, Naishee walked in without caring about the eyes on her, or on her forearm to be exact. Before entering DK's cabin, she turned and shouted back at the ones who were talking behind her back seeing the tattoo, 'What? Can't I tattoo whatever I want? It's my body.' She entered DK's cabin and stopped. She was with a young employee. She was kneeling on the ground and he was on the couch beside her table. That corner was the only part hidden from the two glass walls of her cabin.

'I'm sorry,' Naishee said and was about to leave when DK stopped her. She gestured to the younger guy who stood, tugged his trousers up and left hurriedly. Naishee had seen him once or twice before in the office. He was a new recruit.

'Please don't—' DK started but was cut short.

'DK, it's your office. Do what you want. I'm not going to rat you out in front of anyone and you know it. Just one request. Please don't destroy my image of you like this. It's not that we get an inspirational woman every day in the workforce.' Naishee's voice had a certain earnestness that hit DK hard. It almost embarrassed her.

'You're right.' DK went to her desk and settled down holding her head.

'I need to pull my socks up. This can't go on this way,' she was talking to herself. She lifted her head and looked at Naishee who was still standing where she was.

'What brought you here?' DK asked.

'I wanted to cancel my Pune shift, and request you not to drop me there.'

'Why, what happened?'

'The man for whom I wanted to shift and do my bit to keep the relationship going couldn't take this,' she flashed her forearm. DK stared at the tattoo.

'Why would you tattoo such a thing?' She was taken aback.

'Exactly. That's what he should have asked. No girl would tattoo such a thing on herself. But guess what, I think people don't have time to invest in people. They have all the time to invest in love. Not people.'

There was silence.

'All right, I'll keep you here.'

'Thanks, DK.' Naishee left the cabin. DK sighed. What remained with her were Naishee's words. *Please don't destroy my image of you like this. It's not that we get an inspirational woman every day in the workforce.* DK picked up her phone and opened her camera. She switched on the front cam and looked at herself. *Why didn't he think of her the way a girl much younger than her had just told her?* She had a bad life, a bad past. But what Naishee caught her doing was reckless. Was something below her dignity. Was something out of pure desperation. Naishee was right. Successful people like her have a responsibility that should drive them to go beyond their own petty excuses to be sad in life. DK was going to have her menopause soon. But did that mean she would stop being a woman? She understood it was up to her to begin life anew after her fifties. Make a fresh bucket list perhaps. Live her freedom of not being bracketed as a sexual object by society. DK saw her image had a smile now. There was a sudden rush of positivity. Of hope. She opened her WhatsApp and went to Naishee's chat window. She typed and sent a message to her.

Thanks Naishee. Don't ask me why. Just 'thank you'.

Naishee read it and sent a couple of hug emojis.

Two days went by. Naishee was expecting some communication from the kidnapper. Should she keep the tattoo? Or mask it? Or show it to anyone in particular? The first day was embarrassing. But then the stares stopped bothering her from the second day. A mere tattoo couldn't define her, just as a few accusatory stares wouldn't prove any guilt. Nothing came from the kidnapper. It did affect her peace of mind, though. From the third day, the sight of her own tattoo was irksome to her. It reminded her that from the time Shravan had been kidnapped, Naishee seemed to have been running in fifth gear all the time, with no rest. And considering whatever she had gone through, there was still no guarantee that she would get to see Shravan alive ever again. There was only hope. Sometimes that's all one needs. Sometimes even that doesn't help make the cut.

Naishee went home dejected. It was one of the most unsatisfying days at work. Not because of the work but because of her own mindspace. The goings-on in her life had turned her into someone fastidious at work. And irksome.

Not able to hold back any more, Naishee shot an email to herself assuming the kidnapper would read it sometime.

Would you care to tell me why have you subjected me to so much punishment? What's your motive? What's your kick? Making people suffer is fun for you?

She emailed it. It was after she finished having some soup at night and had retired to bed that Naishee saw an email from herself. It was the kidnapper. He had not only read her email but replied as well. This was the first time the kidnapper had communicated without any exam question, but it did have an activity at the end of it. The email read:

I too made the mistake of assuming it all to be punishment. It's not. In reality, it's all a preparation. For what, you may ask. You'll know soon. Your final question will answer it for you. Till then, go and slap the one person you respect the most and attach the video here.

Slapping the person she respected the most? DK? Or . . . Naishee checked herself. She respected her parents the most. This didn't seem that difficult compared to the rest. She could always apologize to her parents and explain to them what the situation was. And what triggered the action. Could it be this easy? *There had to be a catch somewhere*, Naishee wondered. She booked her bus ticket to Karur for the day after since she had an important work assignment to complete the next day.

While Naishee was reading the mail and weighing the feasibility of her next action, in Mumbai Ashwath was wondering if he should call Naishee and inform her. He had received a parcel with a mobile phone, the same as the ones Naishee had received multiple times by now.

A minute of thinking hard, and Ashwath decided against informing Naishee. The content of the video on the phone was too much to take the risk of upsetting the sender.

* * *

Chapter 25

Mani Kamaraj was at a grocery shop when he saw a car come to a halt in front of the store. He couldn't see who was inside. He bought whatever he had to and moved out of the store. Since the time he had come back from Bengaluru with his wife, his shoulders had drooped. And he had started looking older and weaker than he did before. He began walking towards his house with the grocery bag in hand. A little later, he noticed that the car that had stopped at the store was following him. He stopped and turned to look directly at the driver. He adjusted his specs a little and then a smile appeared on his face.

'Ashwath,' he murmured to himself. Mani went to the car. Ashwath smiled at him.

'Come, uncle, I'll drop you,' he said.

Mani quickly got into the car and turned to put the grocery bag on the back seat.

'How come you're here, son?' Mani asked. 'Where's Naishee?'

'Naishee is in Bengaluru. I came here for some work, uncle.'

While chit-chatting, Ashwath drove to a different location. He parked the car in front of a brick wall where some political graffiti had been drawn.

'One second,' said Ashwath, stepping out of the car and gesturing he needed to pee. He went behind the brick wall. But didn't emerge for more than a minute. Mani kept waiting in the car. He did notice Ashwath seemed a little nervous since he had sat beside him in the car. Had anything happened between Naishee and him? What work would Ashwath have in Karur? As far as he knew, he didn't have any relatives or family here. Mani took out his phone from his shirt pocket and was about to call Naishee when he heard Ashwath calling him urgently for help. Sensing some trouble, Mani stepped out of the car quickly and went behind the brick wall. He couldn't locate Ashwath. As he turned, he felt a blunt object hitting his head. Before he knew it, Mani fell unconscious. Ashwath looked around. There was no one there. It was a lonely road, but it was daytime. Anyone could walk by or bike by. He held Mani by the legs and pulled him towards the car. He managed to put him in his car's trunk and then quickly drove off from the place.

As Ashwath drove out of Karur, he went past a bus that was coming into town from Bengaluru. Naishee was in it. She was too lost in her thoughts to notice Ashwath's car. She reached Karur bus stop and went straight home. It was Meenakshi who opened the door.

'Where's appa?' Naishee asked.

'He has gone to the grocery store, must be on his way back. What happened?' Meenakshi sensed something was up.

Naishee came in. She didn't tell her mother anything. The two ladies waited for Mani to return but he didn't. Growing impatience made Naishee go to the grocery store herself to inquire about him.

'He was here. It's been three hours. He left taking all his stuff. Hasn't he reached home?' The storekeeper too sounded concerned.

Naishee reached out to some of Mani's friends in Karur, as well as a couple of their relatives. But Mani was nowhere to be found. Inquiring at every home in the locality and coming up with no information, Naishee's heart started beating faster. Had Mani too been kidnapped? She rushed to the police. But she was told the usual. To wait for twenty-four hours. It was while she was coming back that she met Anju George—a lady from the locality. She was a loner who used to give private tuitions to kids. Both Naishee and Shravan had studied under her at some point.

'What happened, Naishee? How come you're here in the middle of the week?' she asked.

'Appa is missing.'

'Missing? I saw him in a car.'

'A car? Was he driving?'

'No, he wasn't driving. He was sitting in front. Someone else was driving. I don't know who.'

'When was this?'

Anju George thought for some time and said, 'Been two or three hours for sure.' A worried-looking Naishee rushed away.

Ashwath reached the place asked of him in the phone's video. A spot near the highway between Karur and Bengaluru. He parked the car. There was no one in the vicinity. He stepped out and went to the car's trunk. Mani was still unconscious. He pulled him out. Ashwath had brought tape using which he bound Mani's hands, legs and mouth properly, and left him by the highway. That was also asked of him. He took a turn and drove off to Chennai instead of Bengaluru. In between his drive, he called home.

'Appa, is there any news of mom?' he asked.

'She was found unconscious on the road a while back. People are getting her home. What happened? How did you know she had gone missing?'

'I'll come home and let you know. I'm on my way to Chennai.' Ashwath hung up and stepped on the accelerator. He felt relieved.

Naishee came back home with nothing on Mani. Meenakshi started crying seeing her that way.

'First your brother, now your father. What bad thing have we done to anyone to deserve this from god?' Meenakshi was uncontrollable.

Naishee went to her room and locked herself inside. She needed to think objectively, bereft of emotions. Her gut told her this was connected to Shravan. She checked her email. There was no intimation from the kidnapper. Until he emailed, she would not know if her gut was absolutely correct. Evening came. Naishee thought that perhaps the email wouldn't come if she didn't comply with the kidnapper's demand. She went downstairs with her phone video on, slapped her mother hard, stopped the video and apologized, giving her a peck on her cheek.

'I'm sorry, amma. I'll explain later,' Naishee said and then came back into her room like a whirlwind. Meenakshi stood puzzled. She thought she had dreamt the entire episode. Upstairs, Naishee attached the video and sent the email to herself. She kept the email screen open on her phone. Half an hour later, the email was accessed. And a reply came in the form of a location along with a demand: She had to bring someone to the spot whose location was given. And that someone was . . . Ashwath's father. Naishee could not make heads or tails of it.

Meanwhile, after Ashwath had left an unconscious Mani by the highway, two burly men came out from the adjacent forest and lifted him up without being noticed by anyone. They took Mani inside the forest, put him down at a particular point and waited. After a good two hours, the orphan lady came to them. By then the men had dug the earth in the form of a grave near the spot where they had placed Mani. As the orphan lady arrived on the scene, the men got busy burying the still unconscious Mani up to his neck. Only his head was left to be buried. From some metres away, Shravan, his mouth stuffed with a cloth, could see it all. Seeing his father being buried, he feared that his entire family would be brought there, one by one, and they would be buried alive . . . together.

* * *

Chapter 26

This was impossible. How would she get Dushyant to the location? He hated her. He would never agree to it. And she couldn't possibly tell him all that had happened in the last few months. Unlike the other activities that the kidnapper had asked for or subjected Naishee to, this one was different. She couldn't possibly pull this off without any consequence to her person in life. Living in the container, tattooing SLUT on her forearm, standing as a human lightning conductor—they were all about her. The other activities were about humiliation, embarrassment and psychological horror; was this one about being insulted, knowing what Dushyant thought of her? For this wasn't about her alone. This involved the father of the boy she was in love with. Maybe they were going through a bad phase in their relationship, but they hadn't called it quits. But if she pulled this off and his father was hurt in the process, it may well be the end of whatever Ashwath and she had between them. But what were her options? A thoughtful minute later, she answered herself: zilch.

Naishee understood that it wasn't the time to think, it was time to act. If she had to reach Shravan and rescue him alive, she would have to do this. Perhaps this was the last act before getting to her brother. No question had come till now so she couldn't be sure. Perhaps completing the activity successfully would qualify her for the last question. Naishee promised her mother that she would get her father back soon and asked her to take care of herself. She took a train to Chennai. She knew where Ashwath lived, though she had never been to his place.

It wasn't much of a challenge to locate Ashwath's house. The good thing, Naishee thought, was that he wasn't at home. She went inside the main gate and pressed the doorbell. Dushyant opened the door.

'Hello, uncle.'

'Naishee? What are you doing here?' Dushyant was not only surprised but there was a hint of irritation too on his face.

'Ashwath told me—'

'Oh, so he told you about his mom. Come in.' He went inside leaving the door open. Naishee followed him, closing the door behind her and checking to see if anyone was inside besides Ashwath's mother.

'She is asleep. So, you have to wait till Ashwath arrives,' Dushyant said.

'What happened?'

'Ashwath's mom was missing for a couple of days and then was miraculously found lying by the roadside.'

'Miraculously? As in?'

'I mean she suddenly appeared there. She has minor injuries, but everything else is all right.'

'Who could have done this?' she asked.

'How do I know? I'm waiting for Ashwath. Once he arrives, I will talk to the police. I had lodged a complaint but so what if she's back? I won't let the perpetrator go scot-free.'

There was silence. Was Ashwath's mother Remya's going missing related to both Shravan and her father going missing? Naishee realized this wasn't time to try and deduce anything. If Ashwath arrived there, then she wouldn't be able to carry out the plan she had come up with.

'Uncle, may I have a glass of water, please?' Naishee asked. She watched him get up and go to the kitchen. Naishee took out the hammer she had brought with her. On her way to Chennai, she had read up on Google where to hit a person so he fell unconscious immediately. She sauntered to the kitchen behind Dushyant.

Dushyant, with his back to her, was pouring water into a glass from the purifier. Naishee tiptoed up to him and then, aiming at his spine, hit him with all her might. Dushyant immediately collapsed to the floor, unconscious and grunting slightly. She switched off the purifier. The fact that Ashwath's mother hadn't come into the kitchen told her she indeed was asleep. Naishee put the hammer back in her bag and tried pulling Dushyant out. She realized she wouldn't be able to pull him alone. He was too heavy. She hadn't planned for this. What should she do? She looked around, thinking hard. Her eyes went to the cooking gas cylinder. It had a tray with wheels below it. If there was a cylinder at work, there had to be another empty one.

It didn't take Naishee long to track the empty cylinder that had a tray with wheels below it. It was placed there so that the cylinder could be moved around the house easily. Naishee took out both the trays and placed them on the floor. With all her energy, she managed to get Dushyant to stand up and put his feet on each tray. Supporting his body with one hand around her shoulders, which was easier than pulling him, Naishee took him to the main door, moving him on the wheeled trays. She picked up the car keys from the key holder beside the main door before going out.

She unlocked the car and put Dushyant down on the backseat—he was literally lying there on his tummy. She then pulled the lever to open the car's trunk. As she put him inside,

Dushyant half went in on his own. She put his legs inside quickly and locked the trunk.

Getting into the driver's seat, she checked the location she was sent to take Dushyant to. It was showing a good 236 km away. Naishee drove to a nearby petrol pump, filled the tank and took off for her destination.

Ashwath reached home and was immediately suspicious on seeing the main gate open. He noticed that his father's car wasn't in the small parking space beyond the main gate. He went further in only to notice the main door was open too. Ashwath was on the alert, in case there was an intruder. As he tiptoed inside, nothing seemed out of place. He relaxed on seeing his mother. The parcel sent to him had the video of his mother tied to a chair, with a man putting a dagger at her throat. The demand was simple and straight. If he didn't bring Naishee's father to a specific location, his mother would be killed.

His mother smiled weakly on seeing Ashwath. Clasping her hands, he told her to get some rest. He went around the house but couldn't find his father. He dialled his number only to realize his phone was on the couch. He came to the bedroom and asked his mother about Dushyant. She had no clue.

'He told me he was waiting for you to come home,' Remya said.

Ashwath went out to the hall room and called Naishee. She picked up at the second ring.

'Yeah, Ash.'

'Where are you?'

'Bengaluru, why?' She tried to stay as calm as possible.

'Did my father call you?'

'Me? No . . . why?' Naishee hated to lie to Ashwath but she had no option. She had been badly cornered.

146

'Nothing. Talk to you later.' Ashwath ended the call and decided to approach the Chennai police.

Naishee reached the location after four hours of continuous driving. There was no way she could take the car inside the forest. Still, she took a left, entered it and drove as far as the curvy, stony and rough path permitted her. She didn't want to leave the car lest some police patrol noticed it. She was sure Ashwath would have gone to the police by now.

She stopped the car realizing she couldn't go any further in it. Naishee stepped out to open the car's trunk. She tried her best to get Dushyant down but she wasn't able to. She suddenly saw two burly men in front of her. Naishee's heart missed a beat. They talked in Tamil as they respectfully asked her to step aside. She did. The men came up and lifted Dushyant out. She watched them carry Dushyant for some distance to where two shovels were kept. They dug the earth as Naishee, with her feet frozen on the ground, watched in silence and horror. They buried Dushyant to his neck. Only his head remained to be buried. Then the two men left.

Naishee kept screaming behind them to take her to Shravan but they didn't bother. She even ran and tried to stop the men. They pushed her and disappeared from sight. As Naishee fell, she was slightly injured. Before she could get up, she noticed a source of light from the side where Dushyant was buried. But instead of him, the light source highlighted Mani and some distance from him was . . . Shravan—hands tied, half buried in the earth. But alive.

* * *

Chapter 27

Naishee's first instinct was to run to her brother but a voice stopped her.

'Wouldn't you like to meet me first, Naishee?'

She turned to see Anju George.

'Anju ma'am?' Naishee said aloud incredulously. Seeing her there, images of Anju George from the past started flashing in front of Naishee. She not only lived in their locality and had given tuitions to the siblings, but Anju George had also come to their house several times during her or Shravan's birthday celebrations. Though she was only thirty-two, she looked older than that. She was on the obese side, wore spectacles and as far as Naishee knew, didn't have any family.

'What are you doing here, Anju ma'am? What's all this about?'

Anju smiled in a diabolical manner. Naishee realized this was the first time she had seen her smile. She always had a stoic face. In fact, Shravan and she had joked several times about how emotionless she looked.

'This is about two monsters and their little sport,' Anju said.

'What do you mean?' The same woman who seemed completely harmless, coy and soft was now looking menacing with only one half-smile hanging on her face. So much so that Naishee could feel her throat go bone-dry with every second.

Anju George was wearing a dress covering her from neck to heels and sports shoes. Anju slowly pulled her dress up, exposing her right leg. As she did so, she noticed a big tattoo there: VECI (SLUT). The same word that was tattooed on Naishee's forearm. The latter's jaws slowly fell open in disbelief.

'It's not the tattoo alone that is common to us. There's more, Naishee. Wouldn't you like to know?'

Naishee moistened her dry lips in anticipation. It took Anju George around fifteen minutes to sum up her life's story from the time she came to Gita Vidyashram, Vellore, from the sister orphanage in Nellore until she saved Arpita from the two monsters. The uncanny resemblance to what Anju George had to go through at the hands of the two beastly teachers and the activities that she had subjected Naishee to, made her guts churn. Naishee felt she could throw up at any time.

'This tattoo was the punishment they gave me for raising the alarm about Arpita,' Anju George continued. 'Though Arpita eventually was saved, my life was ruined. My character was assassinated wherever I went. My school didn't allow me to sit for my standard ten exams. You know what's the most disturbing of all sounds, Naishee? When your dreams come crashing down but not of your own volition. You never recover. My dreams weren't very high or complicated. They were simple. I just wanted to come to the city and live. Live like a human being. Not as an animal, not like some filth, not as someone's sadistic sport.' Anju George took a long breath and said, 'You must be wondering, if I was subjected to shit then, how does it matter to you? Of course it does. You have the same genes as that of one of the perpetrators.'

Naishee already had a bad feeling about this. She knew whatever was coming next from Anju George could scar her for life.

'The history teacher is none other than your father, Mani Kamaraj. The science teacher is Ashwath's father, Dushyant Iyer,' Anju George said.

Naishee couldn't believe what she had heard. She felt her knees getting weak. She collapsed on them. And sat still.

'You know, when I was chucked out of school, the obvious thing for me was to move away. Go someplace else where nobody knew me or my scars and settle there. Guess what I did. I stayed back in Vellore itself. A different locality. But every day, I kept an eye on Mani and Dushyant. Even when they shifted to Chennai after getting a lucrative offer to teach in a private school there. Dushyant settled in Chennai. Mani, however, came to his hometown in Karur and settled there after his wedding. I came here following Mani because everything started on that fateful day I said the correct answer in front of the invigilator and faced Mani's wrath. Can you imagine this, Naishee? I answered correctly and fucked my own life up.'

Naishee could sense from her voice how self-debilitating the ordeal must have been for Anju George. And knowing that the monster was none other than her own father was . . . Naishee would have done anything to have someone erase this moment from her life.

'What if . . .' Naishee felt her voice shaking, 'what if you are lying? My appa isn't a monster. I don't know who you are talking about.'

'You can ask both Mani and Dushyant when they come to senses if anything of what I told you is wrong. You can talk to any old staff in Gita Vidyashram as well. But it hardly matters to me whether you believe it or not. People are born evil, Naishee. I think Mani changed a little only after you were born to him. A daughter. He realized men would look at her the way he looked at women, hence he was always protective.'

'And you waited these many years because you were looking for an opportunity for revenge?'

'I had plenty of opportunities to do whatever I wanted to do with him. But I waited. Because I wanted to strike at a time when he was most vulnerable. Just as he had struck me when I was most innocent. But I didn't want to only kill him. No. I wanted to stretch the story. If I had married and had kids, I'm sure my scars would have affected their upbringing. A scarred parent can rarely have a healthy child. And I'm not talking biology here. You getting it, Naishee? Your father had not only injured me but also my ability to keep any progeny of mine happy too. That's one principal reason why I never married.'

'So you wanted to fuck his daughter and son up as well?' Naishee said, turning to glance at Shravan. He was lying quietly in fear at some distance. He could see his sister and Anju George were having a conversation.

'So, Naishee, as I said,' Anju George began, 'things that happened to you weren't punishment. It was preparation. I wanted you to go through and experience what I did. Maybe not to the extent I did because I'm not a monster like these two. Also, you are an adult and I was a child. There's a world of a difference; still I wanted you to feel me. Understand me. Know me. They say if two people undergo the same kind of trauma, pain and suffering, they begin to share an unspoken bond. You don't know this, Naishee, but we are bonded already. And it brings me to your last question of twenty-five marks in the exam. You have to score full marks in this. The question is simple and needn't be answered using words. Answer it with action. Remember how in school we have theory and practicals. This is the latter. So, here's the question: Now that you have lived what I went through at the hands of your father and his friend, what do you think—who should live? Shravan or these two? You can choose only one. And I know whom you will choose. My choice of you wasn't random. I studied you more deeply than you can fathom. Of course, you can hand me over to the police now that you know my identity. But I feel my purpose is done for this life. Whether I die or spend time in jail, I don't give a damn. You're free to do whatever, but after you make the choice. I mean, you can choose both as well, since one choice involves your father and would-be father-in-law, but if you do that, you'll live your life more with hatred than with love now that you know your father isn't the hero you thought he was. He is a beast you never knew.' A pause later and she added, 'I repeat myself, Naishee, you were wrong. Human beings are born evil. Only few—very few—manage to turn and become good. Whoever you choose should live, you can leave with, and my men will bury the other alive. And if you release all three here, my men will make sure you four would be buried alive.'

Anju turned and slowly walked away. Naishee noticed the two burly men appear again.

An hour later, only two people walked out of the forest. One was Naishee and the other was Shravan. Half an hour after Anju George left the place, Dushyant first came to consciousness. He was scandalized to find himself dug in a grave with Naishee in sight. He thought she had gone crazy. He kept first ordering, then pleading with her to let him go, but she didn't. It was only when Mani came to consciousness that Naishee went to him.

'What's all this? Get me out of here.' Mani somehow managed to speak. From the corner of his eye, he noticed Dushyant in the same predicament. The latter had seen him too. Naishee clenched her jaws and asked, 'Appa, did you both teach in Gita Vidyashram, Vellore?'

'Why are you—'

'There's no time, appa. Just answer me.'

'Yes, Dushyant and I used to teach there, but a long time ago. Even before your birth.'

'Did Anju George study there?' Naishee asked and saw her father's face turning pale.

'I told you to kill that bitch long ago, Mani. Now she is screwing us over,' Dushyant yelled out. And that was it. Naishee didn't need any other validation or proof. She started weeping.

'Listen, Naishee, whatever happened, happened. We can't erase the past but we can apologize if that's what you or Anju want. I'm sure she must have filled you up with nonsense about us but—'

'Appa, shut the fuck up!' Naishee shouted. That was the last thing she said to Mani. She didn't even care to look at Dushyant.

Naishee and Shravan reached the highway on foot, guided by one of the burly men. They found a police van waiting there. The police came walking towards them along with Ashwath. The latter spotted her first and ran up to her.

'What are you doing here? Where's your father?' he asked.

'My father? Must be at home. I came here to rescue Shravan. This is my brother,' Naishee said, holding Shravan tight by the arm. Ashwath looked at Shravan, then at Naishee. Nothing made sense. One of the police officers came up to them.

'We are looking for Dushyant Nair. Have you—'

'No, sir. I just came to get my brother.' She turned towards Ashwath and asked, 'What happened to your father?'

'He is missing,' the police officer said instead. 'But what are you and your brother doing here?'

'It's a long story, sir. Right now I'm just happy to have my brother alive beside me. I'll tell you everything in detail but we need to go to my mother in Karur,' Naishee said.

'No problem. Our vehicle will drop you home. In fact, you can fill us up about all this during the drive.'

Naishee and Shravan shared a look.

'Sure. I don't mind, sir,' Naishee said.

The police officer asked a few of his men to search the place, for Ashwath had told them he had dropped Naishee's father there. The police officer understood she didn't know about that yet, hence he didn't say anything to her face. He rather wanted to know what her story was.

Ashwath, Naishee, Shravan and the officer got into the police vehicle. From here, Naishee knew, it would be a long, long journey.

Epilogue

The Right One

Meenakshi could hear her children laughing out loud. She was in the kitchen, standing by the stove, waiting for the milk to boil. The kids had demanded some steaming coffee. Meenakshi, along with Shravan, had shifted with Naishee to Bengaluru. Months had gone by since the time Naishee had come to Karur with Shravan. All she told Meenakshi was that Mani was nowhere to be found. When Meenakshi took the coffee mugs to the hall room where the kids were, she noticed they were watching Ashwath's stand-up comedy stint on an OTT platform on television. She placed the mugs on the centre table and sat down beside Naishee.

'How is Ashwath doing?' Meenakshi asked.

'I don't know, amma. I told you we broke up. When people break up, they don't usually know what the other is up to in life.'

'You tell me that all the time but never tell me why you broke up.'

'Amma, we just weren't going good. He had to be in Mumbai and I couldn't be there. It wouldn't have worked out,' Naishee said and got up. She went to her bedroom to change out of her shorts. In reality, she had broken up with Ashwath for obvious reasons. Ashwath and his mother still knew, just like her mother, that Dushyant and Mani were missing. Naishee had slowly made it clear to Ashwath that it would not work out between them. Even he didn't show any resistance. It did surprise her because Naishee had neither told him nor the police anything about their respective fathers or Anju George or anything that connected Shravan to their going 'missing'. But she didn't care much any more. She did love Ashwath, but she knew the love wouldn't be able to override the impact of the information.

Till now, eleven months since the day she saw both their fathers being buried alive, Naishee used to think about Anju George's story. She used to get gooseflesh imagining what she must have gone through because of her father. Growing up, Naishee thought Mani was the most caring and loving person. She never knew he was a legit paedophile. How does anyone absorb such a fact about one's father? She couldn't even miss her father for she knew the one who parented her perhaps wasn't her father at all. Or maybe he was just a small part of it. At times when she saw her reflection in the mirror, she wondered if his blood was really running in her veins. Was she too as evil as him? The thoughts had made her amazingly tolerant in the last months. It was as if she was looking at the world and people in a different manner altogether than she used to.

Naishee went to the hall room, having changed from shorts to trousers, and told her mother, 'I'm getting the vegetables. You need anything else?'

Meenakshi didn't need anything. Naishee went downstairs to the vegetable guy outside her apartment's main gate. As she was picking the veggies, Anju George drew the curtain of her bedroom from the apartment opposite. When she got to know the mother and children were shifting places, she was disturbed. Within a month she understood she wouldn't be able to live without seeing them. She had been keeping an eye on the family for a good twenty years. And old habits die hard. They had become her family in the most twisted way possible. And now she couldn't live without them. She needed to keep them on her radar. As Naishee went back to her apartment after buying the vegetables, Anju George drew the curtain tight.

She went to the table where she had kept a small bottle. She stuffed her mouth with a cloth so no scream would come out. Then poured the contents of the bottle on to her tattoo. As the acid burnt her skin, she screamed her lungs out. She could bear a skin scar, but the scar that the tattoo had inked on her soul . . . it was time to free herself of it. And look forward to new beginnings.

Acknowledgements

After writing the sequel to my previous romantic thriller, I was keen on writing an out-and-out thriller without a heavy dose of romance or relationship philosophy. Just a cut-to-the-chase kind of fast-paced story. I hope my readers enjoy a subtle detour from my signature style and finish this in one go. That was the intention, to begin with.

Heartfelt thanks and gratitude to the ones who played an important role in this journey of mine:

Milee Ashwarya—thanks for always believing in my stories. Can't thank you enough for everything. Cheers!

The marketing and sales team—for helping me reach my readers each and every time.

Ralph—for the smooth copy-edits.

My readers—for showing love and appreciation always. You guys are my strength and motivation.

Friends, family and Ranisa—for being there whenever I need you all.

R—for making me a better version of myself. Deeply indebted.